A World of his Own

Stephen Hirst

I love this book!
Ben

Contents

To Bramblingums everywhere

With thanks to Stowe for inspiration and support, and especially for allowing the use of their buildings and grounds as a setting, although Brambling College is not, of course, Stowe School, and the events and characters of this novel are fictitious. For reading and encouragement many thanks to Steven Thompson, James Cooke, Ben, Tris and Jamie Hirst; to Sue Rowland for the cover artwork and to Sheila for, well, for everything, as ever.

Tork

"If the whole of western society could just start again, then it would be somewhere like here that it would happen – and that should mean something to you."

Tork left an eloquent pause which Mike attempted to steal by spreading his hands in disbelieving hopelessness and catching the eyes of the casual audience around.

"It doesn't mean anything to anybody because it doesn't even make sense..." Mike swivelled his eyes back to focus on Tork again, but Tork had used the pause better: he had left. "Oh, fine – just come out with a piece of meaningless drivel then exit dramatically." Mike chucked his pen on the table in a gesture just too restrained and self-conscious for dramatic success. "How does he manage to get away with that stuff? I mean, does he teach like that? Some sort of hypothetical followed by any idiotic remark he wants, then leave the room if necessary?"

Alan was shaking his head a little, but mostly he was smiling. "He's an idealist, Mike – he's never compromised that. I've always sort of admired him for it."

Mike sighed. "Well, I guess I'm not then – put me down in the pragmatic realist camp. Or with the grown-ups, you could say."

Tork left the thwarted Mike in the common room and loped obliviously past his stuffed pigeon-hole of memos. At the door he found two boys loitering.

"Ah, it's young Baffled, or Barracking, or Battered, I see."

"Barratt, sir."

"Quite. That's what I said. Now, Baccarat, when I look at you, what do you think I see?"

"An unfinished seed-drill?"

"Exactly. That's exactly what I see. So?"

Barratt looked oddly pleased about the way things were going. "Well, sir – me and Lyle here were coming to the workshops this afternoon..." He paused.

"But you got lost and ended up outside the common room?"

"No, sir – we need to see Mr McManus to ask to be excused cricket. Do you think that will be alright, sir?"

"What?"

"To miss cricket and come to the workshops instead?"

Tork feigned deep thought. "Hmm. Well, it's a question of priorities, isn't it? Is there an O level in cricket?"

"No, sir!" They both chirped happily.

"And is there a crucial bit of cricket coursework due for an imminent deadline?"

"No, sir!"

"So is it more important to spend the afternoon doing Design or cricket?"

"Design, sir!"

Tork nodded then shrugged. "Sounds like a decision to me." But no sooner had he swept them off in the direction of the workshops than he stopped again. "But wait a minute..."

"Sir?"

"Didn't you want to see Mr McManus?"

"Oh, no, sir – not if you say it's okay." Barratt tried to look encouraging.

"Only polite to ask, though, isn't it?"

Barratt squirmed. "He won't agree to it, sir."

Tork looked confused. "But we decided: it's a logical priority."

There was an awkward silence. "You don't know him, sir – he never gives permission to miss cricket practice. If it was your mother's funeral he'd suggest you only really needed to leave five minutes early."

Tork whistled consolingly. "Nevertheless..." he pushed open the door and spoke far too quietly to be heard beyond the pigeon-holes in the common room. "Okay, McManus, come out and negotiate if you ever want to see these boys in white flannels again." The distant hum of Mike and Alan's conversation died peacefully; somewhere a clock ticked. No McManus appeared. "Okay, Barratt and Lyle: time's up. Who's your housemaster?"

"Bozo, sir."

"What are his feelings about cricket?"

"Honestly?" Barratt asked uncomfortably. Tork nodded. "Practically religious I should say, sir."

Tork whistled. "I'm going to require a pretty damn good seed-drill out of this." Two boys nodded furiously. "Okay, let's go - stick close to me." Hooking his overlong red hair behind his ears, Tork strode away down Sub Street towards the Design workshops. Barratt and Lyle punched the air in silent triumph, slapped hands, and fell into step behind.

The Design Department of Brambling College worked rather well, but nobody from the outside could see how this could possibly be. Entering the usual atmosphere of workshop happy purposefulness, even Barratt and Lyle, smirking unpromisingly at their success in skiving cricket without a matron's chit, got on industriously with their seed-drill. They ended up working far harder than they would have done at McManus' cricket practice, although they retained the euphoria of imagining they had wriggled out of the more arduous option.

Tork abandoned them to their system of aluminium tubes and drifted into what passed for his office, sandwiched between metalwork and carpentry. Alex was trying to get a third-former to complete a simple dove-tail. Tork gazed without commitment at the log-jam of assessment folders and preparatory drawings on his desk, then affected interest in it as he sensed Miles, one of his more promising sixth formers, approaching.

"Sir?"

"Hmmm?"

"Do you remember once you mentioned a special project of some sort?"

Tork turned to look at him, but he didn't go for the bait early. "They're all special in their way, Miles. What do you have in mind?"

Miles looked faintly uncomfortable – he wanted something. "Well, it's just that after my last major project, my father wasn't happy..."

"What?" Tork was aghast. "It was an excellent piece of work!"

"Yes, but..."

"It hasn't broken, has it? Is the plasterboard base holding up to use okay?"

"No. Yes, yes – nothing like that..."

"Well does the photograph make it look better than it is?"

"It looks great. It's an invisible bed, and it comes down and goes away easily, and his office doesn't look like it's got a bed in it."

Tork spread his hands. "Ta-da! Job done! Design brief satisfied." Miles still looked uncomfortable. "So what's wrong?"

"Well, he was a bit shocked at the price of the materials."

Tork waved this detail aside. "So you told him cheaper would have been heavier and less flexible, right?"

"Yup. He appreciates that." Miles grimaced. "But said something about had he known the cost then he'd have built an extension and put a bed or an office in that instead." Tork assumed a sympathetic expression. "So the upshot is I'm not to start building anything until the design is fully costed and approved by him, then that's it." Miles looked glum.

"No modifications after the first drawing, then?"

"Not this time, no."

"So you're not allowed to learn anything? You have to get it right first time?" Miles shrugged affirmatively. "Pretty funny view of education your dad's got there."

Miles let this go. "So I'm grounded as far as ambitious projects go, sir."

"Uh-huh."

"And you once said that you had something really special for the right person, and that if you found the right person, you might even be able to help with funding."

Tork pretended to take a moment to recollect. "Oh, yes – I remember." Now he was the one holding the rod, and he wasn't going to strike early.

"So I wondered if I might be the right person?"

"Would you want to be?"

Miles took this as interview practice. "It's good to be challenged – to have something to stretch for like..." Miles suddenly thought a reference to the Olympics would be too sporty for Tork. "...like being asked by Mr Harker to have a go at Oxford University Entrance for English..."

Tork's face expressed surprise, not unpleasant, at the choice of image. "Although I'm not asking you – you appear to be asking me."

"Nevertheless, being selected would be – I don't know, an achievement in itself, I suppose, and an opportunity."

"Or maybe just a way of getting around your immediate money problem?"

Miles nodded. "There is that. But it's mainly that you've held this up as something special, so I want a go at it."

Tork held his eyes for some time. He decided to wait until Miles looked down – the longer the better. As long as it takes. There.

"It's a generator."

Miles looked up, but he also looked disappointed. "Just that?"

Tork sat forward. "Not just any generator. I want you to imagine that Brambling College campus has been completely cut off from the outside world and has to go self-sufficient for an indefinite period. Build that generator."

Miles counted off his fingers. "Oil will run out. Solar unreliable but maybe possible. We could burn wood for a while – I'm not sure how much we've got on the estate - but may not be able to renew it fast enough? Anyway, we like trees. I don't think we could manage nuclear fission. There's a good flow of water over the cascades..."

Tork dismissed this. "But aided by pumps, so that's no use."

"Oh, yeah."

"What else would be different?"

Miles took a second, then thought of something. "We'd probably be growing some sort of annual crop, so there'd be straw of some sort. And would we have animals?"

"Go think it all through, Miles. Come back when you've a couple of ideas."

As Miles left, Tork punched the air much as Barratt and Lyle had earlier. His eyes were ablaze. Alex watched. He had a curious respect for Tork, like you do for a clever joke that isn't funny. He popped his head around the glass partition.

"Hello – someone's lit your flame again: I can see it crackling under that red thatch of yours."

Tork smiled. "I tell you this, Alex: when anarchy comes and szlachta is the new infrastructure, Brambling will be ready!" Fist aloft, he got up and apparently went home, his pile of unexamined folders still on his desk.

Alex turned to his third-form companion. "I don't suppose you can tell me what a szlachta is, can you?"

Szlachta

Mr Parker's third form English lesson had somehow degenerated into ten minutes' silent preparation of the next thirty lines of Chaucer. It wasn't clear whether this was because of 3C's poor behaviour in response to the proffered discussion of religious satire in *The General Prologue* so far, or because Mr Parker had one last sixth-form essay to mark before the next lesson. Either way, the act of looking up bizarre words of middle English in the back of the book reminded James Redmund (mi) of something else he wanted to know.

"Sir?" Mr Parker looked up a little irritably from his marking. He didn't look up with his body — that was poised to return to his essay — but his eyes peered up over the gold-rimmed glasses. James took that as an invitation to continue. "What does 'slacta' mean?" Mr Parker's brow furrowed.

"What's the word?"

"Slactor, sir."

"Spell it."

"I'm not sure, sir, I think it's s-l-a..."

"Well what line is it on, then?"

"Oh, it's not in the book, sir - I just heard someone use it and Mr Adams asked me what it meant."

The class, sensing blood, giggled a little in expectation of Parker's response. As often, it started cool, calculated and dangerous. "What is the class supposed to be doing, Redmund?"

"Preparing Chaucer, sir."

"And what is the class actually doing, Redmund?"

Redmund, confused, looked around him for inspiration. Everyone was looking at him, except a few who were watching Parker. "They're looking at us, sir."

Parker leant back in his chair and stroked the goatee beard that he had, in fact, shaved off the previous week. The blunder made him lose interest in stretching out the theatre of the moment, and desirous of re-establishing the silence that would enable him to return to his essay-marking.

"While applauding your intellectual curiosity and your desire to be of assistance to Mr Adams, I must point out that there is a time and place for everything, James, and that wasn't it, was it? By way of atonement for your sin and encouragement of your scholarship, I shall expect you to begin the next lesson with a short talk on the meaning and etymology of the word 'slacta', or whatever it was."

Parker returned to his essay. The class, disappointed, returned to Chaucer. Neil Rinton, sitting in alphabetical correctness next to James, leaned towards him and whispered, "Which presumably means that he doesn't know either."

During the flurry of toast, chocolate spread and milk that constituted break in his house at Brambling, James managed to discover that a dictionary was of no use on this, despite his creativity regarding different possible spellings. Double French revealed that a specialised English/French-French/English dictionary had no more to offer. Lunchtime luckily produced Mr Adams in the dining hall, but it turned out he himself had no real idea of how to spell 'slacta' either, nor any idea of who would know such a thing: Tork, the only known user of the word, was not about, and had not appeared in the workshops all morning.

"But," Alex pointed out as he returned to examining his lunch, "you mustn't worry about it. I'll ask Mr Fry myself next time I see him if I remember. It was only an idle enquiry, and I'm not convinced it's always wise to find out exactly what he means anyway."

"Oh. Right – thanks, sir." James did not feel able to explain that Mr Parker's intervention had now given the matter rather more urgency. "But if I did want to find out?"

"You'd have to consult the oracle." Alex's enigmatic mutter was instantly doused in a mouthful of school cauliflower. James wandered back to his own lunchtime companion, Chelmsford Charlie.

"What did you want with the Adams family?"

James sat. "Not him, really – I needed to ask Frankenstein something."

"Ah," Charlie peered at the sausage that had impaled itself on his fork. "I think they've lost him. I had Design this morning – whole place had the atmosphere it gets when the crucial allen key everybody needs has gone missing: sort of mix of panic, bluster and recrimination."

"That's 3A talk – give it to me in plain 3C English."

"He's not in. No explanation offered. I don't think they know where he is either."

"Oh." James mashed his potato hopelessly. "What's 'consult the oracle' mean?"

"It's Classics."

"Only if I don't find out, Floozy Parker's bound to make a real thing of it."

"Slow down, 3C-ite, my 13 plus brain is struggling to forge a connection between the Victor Frankenstein of Design, the Oracle of Classics, and Floozy Parker the English master."

One explanation later, Chelmsford Charlie narrowed his eyes and sucked his fork, claiming that he was going into a Sherlock Holmes-style opium-induced trance. James had no idea what he was on about, as often, but waited anyway. Charlie started to intone:

"They told me, Heraclitus, they told me you were dead; Stories of your life were sent spinning round my head. I told matron I was dizzy and had to go to bed. 'I hope it's not catching,' she muttered, grey with dread. 'No worries, woman – it's just something that I read'."

James looked irritated. "Make sense, will you?" he implored.

"Sure – consult the oracle means ask Heraclitus – in the library."

Heraclitus

Brambling's library was grade one listed, but it was the librarian who was treated as a national monument. Heraclitus had seemed impossibly old for generations, and Bramblingums had been starting rumours that he was finally dead for at least thirty years, which had given birth to his current nickname about five years later. "Good God!" was the standard reply of prospective parent Old Bramblingums returning with the fruit of their loins for a tour of the old place and being told the name of the librarian. "You mean the Latin teacher/housemaster/second master when we were here? We used to think he was more or less dead then!"

"That's probably what *your* father said when he first brought *you* here!" would come the witty reply.

"All three dead from the neck up from birth," muttered Heraclitus, whose hearing and memory were much better than generally assumed. In fact, despite living in the wizened husk of a body, Heraclitus retained almost undiminished hearing, sight, intellect and passion – and these last had always been considerable. He had held virtually every significant post on the staff, including a term as stand-in Headmaster, before being reluctantly reduced to his current role. Unfortunate, but inevitable, as it had become almost impossible to hear him anywhere that had any background noise, even if he wanted you to, which appeared to be less and less often anyway.

As lunch hour drew to a close, Heraclitus was trapping itinerant books and distributing them between a set of boxes with labels referring to the Dewey decimal system, there to remain until someone more athletic – one of the library monitors – became available to return them to the shelves. Although the library had had few visitors in the lunch hour, it was nice to see them go. Period six, with any luck, would see no-one there at all except, perhaps, a couple of neat, studious sixth form girls. They might even need a little help with their Latin, French or English, which would pass the time nicely. He might even be able to tell them something mischievous about their fathers. But instead of any such girls, a round-eyed small boy had come in and, after a brief but uneven struggle with a large dictionary, approached.

"Excuse me, sir." Polite boy. Look him in the eye, then. "I- I can't find a word, sir."

Heraclitus, neck tipped slightly forward as his spine now preferred, gazed through straggly white eyebrows. "Never mind: you seemed to find a fair few there. Keep trying."

James Redmund (mi) looked confused. "Sorry, sir? I – I'm... not sure...?"

Heraclitus nodded. "Ah, yes – now you indeed can't seem to find any words. I see what you mean." He looked around the library shelves. "Did you think maybe you'd lost them here amongst those of the masters? Perhaps a classic took your breath away?"

James let this wash over him and pushed on. "I looked it up in the dictionary but it wasn't there."

Heraclitus leaned a little further forward. "And was that just disappointing, or was it a little exciting?"

"Just disappointing, sir."

Heraclitus nodded again, beginning to remind James of one of those model dogs that sit at the rear windscreen in other people's cars. "Perhaps there's a spelling problem. What's the word?"

"Perhaps, sir – I've only heard the word. It's 'slactor', sir."

"Ah. It will probably be the very last word starting with s that you will find," said Heraclitus, oracle-like.

James grinned cheerfully. "Probably, sir – just my luck!"

Amiable boy. Bit of a fool, though. "No," explained the old man, "it's a Polish word. It starts sz."

James's eyes seemed to open even wider. "You know it, sir? What does it mean?"

Heraclitus smiled tolerantly. "I'm here to assist with your use of the library – not to replace it." He returned to his wandering books. James took a backward step, wheeled to look again at the dictionary shelves, but glanced instead at the clock and thought better of it.

"I'd better go, actually, sir – period six. Will the library be open later?"

"It's not locked before your bed-time."

"Oh, great – thank you, sir. See you later – bye!"

He waved as he left, and Heraclitus was deeply surprised to discover that he had himself raised his hand to answer the salute. Surprisingly amiable boy.

Farm

Tork could not be found that morning because he had been at the farm. He and Paul now sat on bales, drinking the beer Tork had thoughtfully put into the fridge on his arrival, sweat sticking their shirts to their skin and dripping off their noses.

"Great job, Paul – never thought we'd get it done in time."

"Yes!" Paul grinned his simple smile and beamed.

"Beer good?"

"Yes!" Paul raised his can in salute and went back to drinking from it.

Tork closed his eyes as his muscles fluttered after the unaccustomed exercise. Important they got that done before the boys arrived, even though it would have been so much easier with their help. He blew disappointingly warm air across his own face where it removed a drip of sweat from his nose and puffed a dampish strand of flaming hair up from his forehead. He gazed down at his skinny legs where they disappeared into his boots, and then up at several grain stores hidden, largely in plain view, around the yard. It didn't matter if anyone noticed that one or two were grain stores – just as long as no-one twigged that they all were.

"Sorry, Mr Fry."

Tork got up and leaned on Paul's huge shoulders: half a matey thump and half a bit of a wrestle. "Not your fault, Paul – not at all."

Paul nodded fiercely. "Paul's fault! Yes!"

"Shh!" Tork put his face, finger on lips, near Paul's. "Shh. Not your fault, and anyway, our secret. No need for anyone else to know! Our secret."

Paul grinned. "Our secret!" and put his hand up. Tork clasped it.

"Our secret." He left it a moment. "Hey, Paul – what went wrong?"

"Nothing!"

"Damn right! It was just a nothing, wasn't it? Not worth mentioning. Good man, Paul."

Paul, Brambling employee and pastoral project, was not, despite persistent rumour, the illegitimate son of a previous head groundsman, nor of any of the other imaginative suggestions for staff in-breeding that Bramblingums loved to speculate. He was simply a work experience favour for a local special school that had been so successful it had never ended, and Paul had now lived at Brambling for twenty years. Childlike but strong, he was best and happiest employed on the grounds, and was on the school's farm whenever he wasn't required elsewhere.

It had surprised everyone (those interested, anyway) when Tork had agreed to take on responsibility for the farm: Tork had deftly avoided taking on any responsibility, especially if it came with admin, for some years, and his contributions outside Design, notably for the Drama festival, were normally "arty". But the farm was a minority, peripheral interest with a budget out of proportion with its clientele, and an operation that sort of followed a design brief, so it could be seen as suiting him. It also provided him with a ready answer to the "where on earth were you?" question which had dogged his career. And he had forged a real connection with Paul, and kept the farm going for the handful of Bramblingums who needed some other afternoon home rather than the sports fields and arts centres, so that the Head was able to congratulate himself on the success and perspicacity of the appointment.

The 'nothing' that had gone wrong was in fact two nothings – zeros that had somehow been added to an order form for a few bucketfuls of grain. Rahman had been using Tork's computer at the time, testing a rudimentary computer game he was designing on Paul, who had become so engrossed by it that Rahman couldn't get him off it again. By the time Tork got back to printing and sending the order he had been writing earlier, two zeros had somehow appeared on the quantity required. The surprisingly large delivery to the farm was, however, now inventively stored out of sight.

"Wow," said the first of the lads to arrive for an afternoon on the farm, "what's the new storage for?"

Tork unstuck his shirt from his shoulder and stood up. "Oh hi, boys. Well," he waved a hand vaguely at the bins that had been delivered that very morning, "always loads of stuff that needs to be properly stored on a farm – feed, fertiliser, grain – and," a brilliant idea occurred to him, "a lot of it has to be maintained at controlled temperatures and humidity, so NEVER open any of these new bins without asking me first, okay?" The boys nodded. "Tell the others." More nods. "Okay. Go feed the ponies, then."

Alison

"Is there anything you'd like to mention?" Deborah peered up from her diary over her pearls and her tortoiseshell half-moon glasses.

"Oh, er – no. No, I don't think so, thanks." Alison was surprised but quite pleased by the question, which seemed to acknowledge the possibility that her underhousemistress role may one day evolve into that of an esteemed colleague who made distinctive and welcome contributions to the team. Although Deborah had already shut her diary, so maybe not.

"Good. Well. Let's see if Julia can impose order on time today." She looked at her watch. "Fourteen minutes past seven."

"I'm sure she will." Alison's reply trailed off without any real conviction.

"Do you think we'll get any interest in the Coldstream Cup? It seems to me a rather unlikely idea. Much less promising than the Duke of Edinburgh awards."

"Well, I..."

"I mean girls here could so easily do community service and skills then take off on a little expedition of some kind, but doing assault courses and rifle training or whatever it is?" Deborah gazed into Alison's face, fully anticipating a supportive snort at the ridiculousness of the idea. "And swimming in the lake in combat gear?"

Alison nosed cautiously forward. "Kate was interested in joining the CCF, although it didn't happen, of course..."

"Quite!" Deborah supplied her own snort of derision – unfairly, Alison thought. Charles had told her that the CCF Commanding Officer would probably have gone with it if Deborah had pushed, but didn't want the bother if neither Kate nor her housemistress were really committed to it.

"She's got a bit about her, Kate." Deborah made no comment. Alison pushed on, "I wonder if we asked her to see if she could get a team together, she might well get four others quite enthusiastic about it. And she'd be pleased to be given the responsibility – captain of a house team – and to do well and prove herself."

"A House team?" Deborah raised an elegant eyebrow. "If we're going to take the boys on then I'm not sure all that machismo stuff is the right activity. Perhaps chess."

Alison ventured another try. "The RSM seemed quite keen to get the girls involved this year…"

"I'm sure he did!" The room somehow crackled with a charge of naivety laid at Alison's feet, and she shut herself down. Deborah looked at her watch. "Where is that girl?" She got to her feet and opened the door wider so that she could see down the corridor. Julia duly appeared at the far end, but stopped when she saw Deborah waiting for her.

"All present, Miss."

"Thank you." Deborah nodded to Julia and stood aside for Alison to precede her to the dayroom.

"House rise!" Julia's command was followed by the restrained noise of twenty-three girls getting to their feet. Alison smiled at them as she entered, then stepped to one side as Deborah swept in behind her and assumed control.

"Thank you, girls. Please be seated." As the girls sat again Deborah opened her diary at the right page and took out some of the notices that had found their way into her pigeon-hole since the last assembly. "There's a History Society meeting tonight, 'What did Edward have to confess to?'" She paused. "I'm not an academic, of course, but I think the point of the good king's title may have been missed there. 8.40 Ante Room. On Thursday the Debating Society will be disputing the motion 'This House Believes Blue is faster than Red'," her gaze lingered on the note a second more before she shuffled it to the bottom of the collection, "so it will be interesting to see what the speakers make of that. Also 8.40 Ante Room - sign out as usual, of course, for those two events. Then there's a meeting for anyone interested in starting a proper student newspaper, tentatively called *Brambling News*, at six o'clock in the Music Room tomorrow. I think that's something it would be good to have girls involved in. The Philosophy Society meeting this week has had to be cancelled, oh, and the CCF have asked if we would like to field a team for this year's Coldstream Cup." Deborah looked up enquiringly and raked twenty-three faces for any sign of interest. Alison managed to catch Kate's eye and beam encouragingly, but although Kate's eyes flicked sideways towards her friends, nearly all the girls were looking without interest at Deborah or else at their feet. The moment seemed to have passed when Lucy started to speak.

"Uh, Miss..."

"Lucy? You'd like to join in with the CCF?"

A ripple half-way between a titter and a smirk passed over the room. "No, Miss – the one before that. The newspaper meeting. I was just wondering who the notice was from?"

Deborah looked put out by the question. "Does it matter?"

Lucy hesitated. "Well... No. But it helps you guess what the newspaper will be like and whether, you know, it's likely to be – fun, I suppose."

Deborah regarded her coolly. "I'd have thought that it would be likely to be exactly what you make of it, Lucy. Life is generally what you put into it." The girls, many of whom had shown some interest in the answer to Lucy's question, all shared in the slight humiliation of the quasi-rebuke, and lapsed into still quietness. No-one mentioned *The Rag*, and if this was to replace it. "Right. Well, if anyone is interested in the Coldstream cup perhaps see Miss Lawrenson while she's on duty tonight." Deborah looked her way and Alison suddenly realised she was being invited to say something.

"Yes, do," she said.

"One or two housekeeping notices..." Deborah continued as Alison silently bewailed the missed opportunity to say something inspiring and stirring. If only Deborah had given her some sort of warning. She dreamed of what she might have said to whip up some enthusiasm as Deborah spoke eloquently on kitchen tidiness and pride in surroundings.

After assembly the girls filed out to "prep" and Deborah went home to the five-bedroom house on site that she shared with her ex-RAF Officer husband, who was the Bursar of the school. Alison settled prep down walking up and down the corridors, then started a round of visits, popping into each room to see how work was going. Eventually it was Kate's door on which she knocked before entering.

"Oh, hullo, miss." Kate looked up from her desk. Alison sat on the bed.

"How's work?" She nodded towards the desk.

"Oh, fine." She pointed the wrong end of her pen at the handwritten pages. "Just a History essay."

"Not on Edward the Confessor?"

Kate laughed lightly. "No. 'Not my period', as historians apparently always say."

"Quite. I never could do History essays. Not wrong, I was always told, just not the way a proper Historian would view it..."

"But you were good at Maths!" Kate seemed to invest the idea with something miraculous.

"Yes, that was lucky, wasn't it?" They both smiled. "So what about this Coldstream Cup, do you think?"

Kate pushed her chair back a little. "I really don't know much about it, Miss. It's a house competition is it?"

Alison leaned forward. "Yes. The boys take it very seriously, apparently. In fact you already see some house teams out practising after prep – that's for the drill section. I'm not sure how we'd manage that, to be honest, but the rest of the competition seems fun. You have to do the assault course..."

"I'd love a go at that!"

Alison smiled. "...and there's a run where the four of you have to carry two logs, and then you swim and ford your way over a corner of the lake, with a rope to hold on to as you go. It's quite demanding I think, but exhilarating and hugely satisfying if you manage a good result! There's an elaborate scoring system based on times and other things, so we could practise and improve our scores and look for a peak performance on the day! It would be great to have a proper sports team with a competition to train for – it's the one thing I feel you really miss out on, being just the twenty-three of you in a boys' school. What do you think?"

Kate's eyes shone, but she was still uncertain. "We'd never get anywhere near the boys."

Alison was ready for this. "Ah, but apparently the RSM has got hold of some stats with male/female equivalences that he can use to work out a handicapping system. So we'd be in with a chance of beating at least a few of the other houses. How good is that?"

For a moment the two of them were slightly drunk on the excitement of the possibility: it did seem like a tremendous break from the summer slog of exam preparation, being outside running, training, practising, with something else to focus on, hope about, push yourself towards.

"Which of the other girls do you think we could get to trial for the team?" Alison's question broke the spell and Kate felt reality creeping back in. She sank a little in her chair.

"I'm really not sure, Miss. It's the kind of thing they tend to avoid." She was already pushing the whole idea aside.

"But a lot of them were keen on sport at their old schools: Arabella played hockey for her county and Roxy got close to the school athletics nationals, which is amazing. Surely they'd want to have a go?" She tried to hold Kate's eye with a brightly optimistic radiance, but she knew she was pulling away from her.

"Honestly, Miss…" She shrugged her shoulders. Alison flared a little.

"Honestly, what? What is it?" Alison softened her tone and touched Kate gently on the shoulder. "Tell me, Kate. Why won't the girls do any kind of sport properly here? They'd get so much more from the place – like the boys do. I don't get it. I need someone to explain it to me."

Kate sighed. "I don't know, Miss. It's… well it's the boys, I suppose."

"The boys? What have they got to do with it?" Alison had only been at Brambling College since the start of the academic year, but she knew what was coming. It kept coming back to this.

Kate looked at her. "Well, nothing, I suppose. I mean that's what you're thinking, isn't it? And you're right, of course."

Just quietly, Alison commented, "Damn right, I am."

"But – it's hard, Miss. You don't…" She waved a hand vaguely. "It's hard."

They both sighed, looked down, took a moment.

Eventually Alison asked gently, "Are we just talking about comments, here? So-called jokes?" Kate nodded. "So don't put your head above the parapet, eh?"

"I guess so."

Alison kept her voice gentle. "That's giving in to bullying, though, isn't it?"

Kate shrugged, more with her eyebrows than with her shoulders. "There are four hundred of them. And it's their school."

Alison pushed firmly away the trigger of that last remark, which tended to make her too cross for her own good, and kept her attitude sympathetic. "Is it just really patronising stuff about how good girls are at sport?"

Kate agreed, but then seemed to suffer a surge of anger. "Well, no, actually. I mean yes, that's there, but it's not the point. It's the personal stuff that gets you."

Alison wasn't sure she got this. "Personal? But how...?"

Kate looked angry with her, now. "Not properly personal, but... Look, if I'm training in CCF gear, running with a log on my shoulder, and I actually look any good at it, then I'll be in for all the butch lesbian jibes. Or all the ones about the way your breasts move when you run, or the wet t-shirt remarks. The ones about being crap, you can come back from those, train harder, get better. But the constant focus on your... I don't know what to call it...you know, the sexual comments..." She looked tearful.

Alison nodded. "Okay, Kate: I get it. I'm sorry." She smiled sadly and sighed. "Maybe some things are just going to take much longer than I thought." She'd let her eyes drift down, but then looked back up to Kate's face again. "I'm just sorry it'll be too late for you."

Kate smiled. "Don't worry, miss. I don't really mind. I mean the all-girls thing at my last school was getting a bit much too, so, you know. University will be ace."

"Yes – it will. You'll love it. And on that note..." Alison got up and nodded towards Kate's desk.

"Yup – back to the History essay."

"See you later." Alison closed the door behind her and took a moment in the corridor, wavering between helpless fury, a shrug of the shoulders, and a steely resolve to be the fearless one to lead this long campaign, actually more likely to become a timid chipping away at a castle.

The next door on the corridor was Emily's, and there was a slightly fraught atmosphere as soon as Alison knocked and entered. Emily was struggling with a bit of Design paperwork that seemed to require her to produce drawings that showed how a complicated joint worked. Even though it wasn't maths, Alison felt it was quite likely she'd be able to help - it was just a question of geometric rotations and a bit of visualising a flat representation in three dimensions. But as she thought she saw the solution, and actually became quite enthusiastic that they'd probably cracked it, Emily just put her pencil down and stared out of the window.

"Emily? Here – where I'm pointing?" Just a view of her ponytail. "Emily? Hello?" Still nothing. "Emily – what's the matter?" A little shrug of the shoulders. "Come on, Emily, I think we're there: we've cracked it!"

Emily turned back, tears in her eyes. "You may be there, miss – I'm not. I've no idea what you're talking about. I must just be thick or something, because it – it's just a blank. I can't do it. As soon as I sort of approach it everything just blanks out..."

Alison soothed her. "You're not thick, Emily – don't be silly. Why you've done art work and written poems I couldn't even begin to attempt..."

"That's different. This is like maths – I just can't get it, I never have. My mum's the same. Dad says it's a girl thing in the family."

Alison rolled her eyes then checked herself. "Sorry – I didn't mean that. It's just – some men often seem quite happy to encourage girls to believe they're no good at maths, like it's feminine or something. Bit of a bugbear of mine – sorry."

Emily seemed for a moment to be considering Alison's speech. "I just can't do maths, miss. I know you're a maths teacher and everything, but it's just not for me."

Alison desperately wanted to go down several of the byways that had appeared on the conversational map, but decided to be wise and stick to the main route. "Okay. But what I don't get is, if you feel that way, how did you end up doing Design instead of History or something?"

Tears welled up again. "I didn't..." she waved angrily at the drawing on her desk, "I knew I didn't want to do anything like this. They said..." she bit her lip and Alison's sympathies lurched for her, "They said I'd be able to do fashion, but when I got here the Design department said they didn't do fashion – didn't even know there was a fashion option, in fact."

Alison was actually a bit surprised herself. "Fashion? You mean like dressmaking?"

Emily winced. "Well, that's involved, but it's not just cutting and sewing, you know. It's Design. You analyse a need, research what's currently available, and materials, then design the product and make it. It's no different to making garden benches and lamps and all this stuff," she waved at her desk again, "except it's really, really interesting and I love it - and I can do it!"

"Wow," Alison was genuinely surprised, "you make your own clothes? And without using patterns or anything?" Emily nodded. "That's amazing."

A slight, shy smile appeared on Emily's face. "Would you like to see?"

"Would I? Absolutely yes, please!" Alison tried not to overdo the girlie camaraderie, but she was genuinely interested, especially when Emily brought out a large sketchbook full of impressive drawings, each page with a main picture centrally then details around the edges to show the fall of a pleat here, a fastening there. Emily was hugely enthusiastic as she talked them through, needing only the slightest encouragement from Alison, and soon leapt up to take from her wardrobe the finished product that arose from one of the designs, holding it up against herself and still full of explanation of every detail. It was a whirlwind transformation from the cross, despairing girl who'd been sitting at her homework so recently.

"That's just fantastic, Emily. I really mean it. You – you've left me speechless. So good. I'd never have thought someone could just do this, out of nowhere, as it were. Wow."

Emily replied with a modest shrug which failed to conceal the glow of pride and pleasure the compliment had prompted. "Well, my mum taught me a lot, and I was taught some sewing skills, including how to use a good machine, at school. And I've just always been interested in what people choose to wear. And my mum used to give me fashion magazines to play with when I was little. It's just something I've always done, really."

"Well, I know nothing about it, I'm afraid," Alison suddenly felt self-conscious about the way she herself dressed, "as I expect you've noticed!" Awkward little burst of laughter from each of them: best to hurry on. "But it seems to me that you're obviously very, very good at this. And there's a Fashion option in Design, you say?"

"It doesn't matter, Miss – I could do fashion anyway on the syllabus we already do here. You usually get to choose your project and materials. It doesn't have to be woodwork and metalwork and electronics all the time, but it just seems to work out that way."

It suddenly occurred to Alison to ask, "Have you seen Mrs Renshaw – or your tutor – about this?"

"I tried, Miss. Mrs Renshaw said she supposed the teachers might find it difficult to mark my work, but she said she'd look into it for me. Then when I asked again she said she was working on it and not to nag."

Alison nodded and stood up. "Okay. I'll see if I can chase it up for you. I'd better go now, but listen – I really enjoyed seeing your work. It was great. Thank you for showing it to me."

Emily shot her a quick smile and lifted her hand in a little wave as Alison left to head for the houseroom and supervise signing out: it was 8.30 already.

Fiona was waiting for her. "Alright if I go to the History Soc, Miss? I've signed out."

"Bit quick off the mark, aren't you, Fi? I don't suppose Edward will start confessing early."

Fiona looked uncertain for a moment, as if she had forgotten the subject of tonight's meeting, but recovered quickly. "Got to get a good seat, though, Miss."

"Oh? Next to whom?"

Fiona grinned – and wondered if that meant she could go now. She risked it and turned to leave.

"Fiona?"

"Yes, Miss?"

Alison paused. She just needed something to balance her last two conversations. "You enjoy it here, don't you? You're pleased you came?"

"Rath-er, Miss: I love it here!"

"But just for the boys?"

"Miss! No. Well yes, okay – but not just that. You're treated differently here. It's less petty." She left the shortest of pauses. "Can I go now?"

Alison smiled and nodded. Other girls, keen to be out, were arriving and readying themselves with their various excuses to leave the house for an hour or so before curfew or home.

Twenty minutes later 'academic society meetings' had presumably started, and those girls with no specific reason to be out of house had been settled back down into the second half of prep. It was dusk, and glancing out of the window Alison thought she caught the first furtive movement in the classroom buildings around the courtyard in front of the house. Boys. Boys in the shadows. Boys who should be in meetings, or else back in their own houses, but were clearly neither. Instead, they were hanging around the girls' house, trying to entice them out. Alison sighed. Some evenings it was like being under siege, or in a cottage in the woods surrounded by siren-like spirits. At the right moment she would go out and chase them all off. Meanwhile, she deserved a cup of coffee.

Eve

Eve enjoyed the peculiarly luxurious sleep of a parent whose toddler had climbed into her bed and nodded off again. She dozed aware that this was a lie-in free of any anxiety or guilt: Tork was gone and Adds was fine. She could hear her son's regular breathing, even feel it occasionally hot on her face, and knew he'd wake and want something soon enough. Meanwhile she enjoyed the physical and emotional warmth of his nearness, and the sense of the strengthening light promising a good day. Dull days in the gloomy interior of their cottage deep in the Brambling woods could be long, Eve trying to sort out the house and Adds needing entertainment, but sunny days were bliss: Adds was contented and good company, housework was out of sight and mind. Eve dozed, looking forward to such a day starting but also pleased with her temporary reprieve from it.

Adds had spread out then rolled over. Eve started preparing herself for his imminent awakening. Sometimes a little cry would follow, but this morning more likely a sleepy grin. Perhaps he'd tell her to wake up and try and prise her eyes open, or sometimes he'd go and get some toys or books and dump them on her – occasionally they'd catch his interest anyway and he'd play absorbedly with them on the bed, her sleeping presence enough for him.

But this morning it was just kicking the bedding off and lying there. Eve pulled it back, he kicked it off again, and that started a good game which ended with hot breathy tickles, her mouth on his warm tummy as he howled and wriggled. Time to get up.

They wandered through the leafy shadows filtering sun-shapes into the two bedrooms, picking up some shorts and t-shirts on their way to the cooler kitchen. Eve sat Adds with his plastic bowl of soft cereal and made some toast. Bare legs and arms recorded the changes of temperature on the way to the garden, where Adds removed his shorts and pants, then came back to Eve at the door for help removing his t-shirt. She didn't argue: it had cereal milk on it anyway, and it seemed healthier and more natural for him to be naked, it helped with potty training, and she liked watching his beautiful, soft-skinned, little child's body trotting busily round the garden. She slipped back in to wash up and get him a drink while he squatted impossibly intent in his close-up examination of some minute detail of life among the grass roots.

Suddenly Adds was with her, his fast little footfalls accompanying his voice, "Ladybird! Ladybird!" as he showed her the creature crawling on his arm. She knelt to appreciate his find, but it was gone. Adds gave a shriek and a jump and wide-eyed gaze. "Flew away, Mummy, flew away!" Adds gave a dance-like leap apparently expressing the feeling of flying away, and Eve picked him up in a hot surge of maternal love.

"Kiss and a hug for mummy?"

The child accepted the hug unthinkingly then arched his little back to be let down. Then, seeming to take on board his mother's question, he squeezed his arms around her neck and planted a wet sort-of kiss on her cheek before heading back for the garden without a backward look. Later, she would take him for a walk and picnic around "their" woods near the edge of the Brambling estate. Meanwhile, the garden was secure, Eve didn't drive, expected no visitors, and had no commitments: another day stretched out before the two of them like a sleepy summer yawn.

Elizabeth

Elizabeth opened the heavy, baize-covered door and scooped from her handbag the keys for the second door within. Stooping to the lock, she seemed briefly to bow to the word "Headmaster" written on the panelled wood before the catch was freed and the door caved in to her firm push. She liked to be early. She liked a few moments before things got going and, even more, she liked a few moments to settle Nietzsche, her Dachsund, into his "niche", as she often joked. Nietzsche had a little round basket in the corner of the room, from where he would watch the day's proceedings. He would have had a walk at least as long as his legs merited, and a minute's fussing with a single dog biscuit was enough for him to take his post until lunchtime.

Elizabeth adjusted and prepared the Headmaster's reception room and her own desk, remembering to turn the computer on. Her typewriter hadn't needed time to warm up, and she kept it in the cupboard just in case, but she was getting used to the – what was it? – the word processor. She had just opened the diary and was studying the day ahead when there was a knock – more of a scuffle – at the door as it opened: Tork Fry, unkempt to the point where she would have mentioned it to a sixth former, with a huge stack of something in his hand. Elizabeth masked her irritation at having been interrupted just before she was ready, and turned on her best welcoming smile.

"Tork – you're bright and early. Too early for the Head, I'm afraid."

Tork affected disbelief. "The Head? He's not the one running the place: it's you I've come to see." Elizabeth switched her smile to sceptical. It was pretty standard nonsense, and a notch or two short of actual charm, but she warmed almost despite herself. He had a youthful enthusiasm about him that was actually more attractive than polished smooth-talking. "I come bearing gifts." He placed a wad of sheets of waxy paper – actually a single sheet folded back and forth at the perforation lines – with holes down either side and white rectangles adhering to them on her desk.

"Oh, my," she said, "labels! How nice. You *have* been a busy boy." She looked at him. "Printed names and addresses... perhaps you had a typing class? Or a very serious detention for a lot of naughty boys?"

Tork tapped his nose. "My secret who did the typing – the point is, no-one will have to do it again. Perhaps a bit of updating in September, that's all." He leaned forward. "It's on the computer." Elizabeth widened her eyes playfully and cocked her head on one side. "Printed it in about five minutes. Can do it again, if you like – as many copies as you want. Alphabetical, by house, by form, by year group, all of them, some of them, none of them – just say, 'tis done."

Elizabeth's mockery had gone. "Seriously?" She looked at Tork, at the labels, and back again. "No-one ever thinks about it, but this could save us so much work..."

Tork smiled. "I think about you all the time. Just let me know what and when, and I'll send them up."

"I – I don't know what to say. Thank, you, Tork."

"You're welcome." He smiled. "And..."

Elizabeth shook her head and smiled, "There's more?"

Tork took a small cardboard square like an envelope out of his pocket. "If you ever grow tired of your dependence on the Design department, there's this!" He made Elizabeth wait. She leaned a little forward and opened her hands to indicate how agog she was. "Floppy disc. It's all on here. Put it in your computer, select what you want and you can produce your own labels on your very own printer right here."

"Good heavens!" Elizabeth was genuinely taken aback. "I think I'd need help with that."

Tork was beginning to move towards the door. "Tutorials available anytime – you know where I am."

"Oh – that reminds me. Message for you. Nice chap from a film company got put through to me for some reason. We had quite a chat, actually - apparently he's an old friend of yours."

"Prune! He didn't give anything away about me, did he?"

Elizabeth raised her eyebrows. "Of course. I made him tell me everything - it's all in your file already." She stopped. "Prune? Don't any of you have proper names? Anyway, the stuff you ordered from him will arrive in the next couple of days. It'll probably get delivered to the school shop."

"Excellent, thanks."

"He said they had fun making it…"

Tork appeared to ignore the implicit question. "Great, thanks. And by the way, how's the television reception working out? Any more feedback?"

"Oh," Elizabeth took a minute to catch up, "yes – well, no. That is, everyone's pleased – it's definitely better. And the bursar's delighted to be able to take down all the unsightly aerials: apparently some 18th century aesthetes have been giving him such a hard time about it."

"Really? Oh, that's good. So no-one's watching television via their own aerials anymore?"

Elizabeth shrugged. "I don't think so – they've all switched over. Of course you can get those portable sets with their own aerials, but I don't think they're much good here. Poor, crackly reception, like the radio."

Tork was about to say something, but they both heard sounds at the door. Tork pulled it open to reveal a surprised Headmaster. "Archbeak! Welcome to your office and good morning."

Whitley Linklater, MA(Hons) Cantab., Headmaster, blinked, absorbed information, and searched the files of his brain. "Ah, Tork – how are you? And how's Eve and, uh, the baby? All well?"

"Oh, *they're* alright, swanning around in their prelapsarian Brambling woods paradise, but here I am slaving away." He smiled cheerfully. Whitley, careful to hide his surprise at a member of the Design department using the word 'prelapsarian', hesitated just too long. "Must be off! Work to do," Tork's voice hung in the air as the door swung behind him.

Whitley regarded his secretary, who smiled at him. "Curious man," he offered.

Elizabeth assented. "Simply dreadful, bohemian, scruffy man," she confirmed, "but he does get things done – and he's kind." She considered telling him about the labels, decided not.

"Hmph," concluded Whitley. "Housemasters' meeting, I think. Anything beforehand?"

"No, Headmaster. Housemasters and Housemistress at 8.50."

Whitley nodded and went into his office.

Charles

Free period 2, Charles was off for a coffee when he noticed Alison disappearing down the short lane to the school shop. He liked Alison, and there were things he could do at the school shop, so he let his feet change direction and follow her. Not that he was 'after' Alison, exactly, but he wouldn't want to rule it out either. He hadn't actually asked directly, of course, but there hadn't been any mention of a boyfriend. So... Charles just enjoyed the fact that there was even a possibility. He had slipped from one single-sex world to another, and was beginning to realise that if he wanted a partner, he was going to have to make some kind of effort to get involved in suitable activities – the kind he had no particular aptitude for, having had no real experience of them. Amateur dramatics. Choral Societies. But not the school ones. He wasn't even very sure what the activities he sought actually were. And here was Alison, a colleague on the staff. It would just be so much easier. And in his third year at Brambling now, and Alison still in her first, he had got to play the kindly, more experienced and knowledgeable mentor, which had been most agreeable.

Alison had gone into the stationery section, and appeared to be stocking up on chalk, board pens and red biros. "Morning, Alison," Charles boomed, rather, "How are you this morning?"

"Oh, Charles – hello." She rattled some red biros at him. "Just stocking up for another exciting evening in!"

"Ah, marking: the pile that just keeps on growing."

"Especially after a busy night on duty..."

They discussed the trials of duty evenings, academic societies that didn't take proper attendance lists, interrupted attempts at marking, and the over-reliance of senior housemasters on their junior colleagues to go to any source of noise after lights-out.

Flight-sergeant Ken Toup, who ran the school shop, drifted off to the stockroom.

Eventually, Alison explained her difficulties with boys in the shadows.

"The sixth formers who don't do much – you know, they're not in the first teams or the lead roles of the school play or – you just don't see them around doing things much - well they know that I don't know who they are. I don't know their names or what house they're in. And I mean, they're a bit like half-trained dogs, you know? If they're quite close to you then they're obedient – so if I asked one as close to me as you are now his name, I'm pretty sure he wouldn't lie about it. But if they're a little distance away, and especially in poor light, they just run. And there's really nothing I can do about it."

Charles batted away the temptation to explain that that wouldn't happen to him, and concentrated on being sympathetic and trying to solve the problem. A rangy, red-haired figure emerged from the stockroom, stuffing some roll-your-own into his pocket. "Morning, Tork," Charles interrupted his own train of thought with a greeting, "stocking up?"

Tork smiled and waved the tobacco. "Just little and often – that's the way. Better go." And he'd gone.

Alison was a little shocked. "He buys cigarettes from the school shop?"

Charles contemplated. "I suppose he hardly ever leaves the campus. Actually..." he furrowed his brow in theatrical thought, "actually he may have your answer." Alison looked surprised. Charles explained. "We did this rather strange house play, and the plot rather depended on this film footage of – well, never mind. The point is, we needed to show something that had supposedly been filmed earlier in the story, and Tork decided it would be much more effective to do it live. So that members of the audience would also see themselves in this footage, you see. He loves stuff like that. And he did it, don't ask me how. But he managed to place a small

41

camera where it wasn't seen, and then replay the film almost immediately, without sending it off to be developed, or anything like that. Amazing the stuff they can do down there."

Alison nodded. "I've never really been down to the CDT workshops, or talked with the staff much. They're sort of separate, aren't they?"

Charles nodded. "Empires within empires."

Alison prompted. "So?"

"Oh, yes, well that could be your answer! If you had one of his cameras on the Nelson House building somewhere, then it could be filming during the bewitching hour, as it were, and you could replay it that very night, get a picture of any particular troublesome wretch, and find out who it was." Charles looked pleased with himself.

Alison was a little uncertain. "Could you do that? I mean even if he would do it for me, isn't it a bit police-state?"

Charles looked hurt. "I don't think that need worry you. And Tork is very co-operative as long as you ask him at the right time, and as long as it's interesting."

Alison stared at the door Tork had used for his exit. "Isn't he a bit – I don't know, a bit too much of a hippy to get interested in security and busting people?"

Charles tutted. "Books by their cover, Alison... So I expect you think he'd have nothing to do with my CCF section, eh? Just not his type of thing?"

Alison shrugged, baffled. "Well, yes – that's exactly what I'd think. I mean not that I know him at all, but he certainly looks more like the Grosvenor Square peace protest type than the military, doesn't he?"

Charles was enjoying himself waving his finger back and forth. "Ah, well, that's just where you'd be wrong, isn't it? Approached the right way, of course, he got very interested and, I have to say, he revolutionised the way I run exercises. And he made them – and my section - much more popular."

Alison was intrigued. "What did he do?"

"Used his drama skills. Happy to tell all - are you walking back for a coffee?"

Alison waved her pens. "Yes – I'll just get these." She managed to draw Ken back out of his stockroom, signed for the pens and turned to see Charles waiting for her by the door. "Wait – didn't you mean to get something?"

Charles lurched. "Yes!" he said, moving forward, "same as you... Just some red biros, please, Ken."

Browning Motion

Chelmsford Charlie was on his way back to Latin period 3 when he saw James exit a cloister and stop dubiously. "Jam jar! How'd it go with Parker?"

James looked to the familiar voice. "I have to find a context."

"For Szlachta?"

"Yes. What does that mean, exactly?"

Charlie switched into an impersonation of his housemaster. "Everything, dear boy: context is everything. It's why you can't wear just your swimmers in the dining hall, even though it's fine in the swimming pool."

James sighed and started walking with Charlie towards Latin, which was the wrong way. "I don't think that helps."

"Should you be coming to Latin?"

"Could your Latin teacher help?"

"Doubt it: 'szlachta' doesn't sound like a Latin derivation. Wrong root. Bit like you: wrong route - as you're not coming to Latin. Here's someone more interested in square roots."

Alison and Charles were coming the other way, taking the short cut past Latin on their way back to the classroom area. "Hello, James," said Alison, "I didn't think anyone in my form did Latin."

James turned round and joined them walking in the other direction. "Hello, Miss. I don't. Just trying to sort something out."

"Oh?"

"I don't suppose you know anything about szlachtas, do you, Miss?"

"Huzzah!" said Charles, rather oddly. They both looked at him. "Probably more History than Maths. It's the sixteenth century name of the Polish/Lithuanian nobility."

James didn't seem either surprised or pleased with this information. "Oh, thank you, sir."

"You're welcome," Charles replied. But he wanted to show Alison that he'd read the signs, "But not solved the problem, eh?"

James shrugged and scratched his head. "I don't think the context makes sense."

Charles needed to wind this up. "Ah, well, I think I've done all History can do. If it's metaphor you want, you'd better ask your English teacher. This is my stop, I think – must dash," and he disappeared into the History corridor.

Alison hesitated before heading back to Nelson House and her marking. "What have you got this lesson, James?"

"Design, Miss."

A fortunate chance: marking could wait. "Design? What are you making?"

James screwed his face up with the difficulty of explanation. "It's not really anything, Miss – it's a dove-tail joint, but it's not a part of anything – just two bits of wood, sort of joined."

"It sounds very mathematical," she said enthusiastically. "Can I see?"

James looked momentarily confused, but recovered quickly. "Of course – you mean now?"

"Why not?"

He shrugged. "No reason."

She smiled. "Let's go."

They walked down past the chapel and the theatre until they found the large, single-storey, apparently improvised building sporting an unfeasibly substantial sign: Craft Design Technolgy.

Alison paused. "What happened to the second o?"

James didn't miss a beat, "It realised it was nothing."

Alison was taken aback as the meaning of this fell fully into place. "James, that was brilliant. What a brilliant reply – and so quick! I can't get over that."

He smiled happily. "Thanks, Miss – but it's kind of standard. They have a string of them, depending on what you say. So if you say 'you can't spell technology' they say 'at least we know what it means'." He looked up. "Oh, sorry, Miss. That would've been a bit rude."

"Good job I didn't say that, then."

"Yes, Miss." James led the way in. Alison had never been in the workshops building before – she hadn't even looked at it enough to notice the sign until now – so she followed him a little apprehensively, conscious of walking into someone else's lesson uninvited, and scanning the place for any sign of a teacher who could reassure her it was okay. She couldn't see one.

The main, central area she stood in seemed a mass of chaotic activity. Fifth form boys were finishing up, pushing stuff back in lockers, leaving stuff out, cuffing or nudging each other into a kind of natural hazard that third formers moved around as they tried to pull stuff out of cupboards and fill up any space at workbenches and equipment that became vacant. Sixth formers drifted in and out, apparently above it all, and with access to rooms off, where they disappeared.

"Hello," a voice behind her said.

Alison turned and saw a bearded, overalled young man holding a large construction of some sort. "Oh, sorry – do you need to get past?"

She moved aside and he leant whatever it was against the wall and turned. "I'm Gareth – technician. Are you alright?"

"Alison Lawrenson," she held out her hand. Gareth went to take it, then waved his in the air instead, to show the oil on it. "Oh – okay!" She put her hand away. "This is my form," she gestured at the third formers milling around, "so I just came to see how they were doing."

Gareth nodded. "That's nice. Alex'll be out in a minute." He nodded towards a door.

Alison glanced in the direction of the nod and back. "Thank you," she said, as he disappeared.

James popped up with his wooden joint. "Here it is, Miss. It's a dove-tail, you see, Miss, because that bit slotted into that bit, and that bit's shaped like a fan. It's a bit wobbly though, but I've filled it up with glue now." He handed it over. Alison examined it.

"It's clever, isn't it? And very well made. And I imagine much stronger than if you'd just glued it, or put a screw through or something. Well done." She handed it back. "So what do you do next?"

James scrutinised his own handiwork. "I have to draw it. But not the gap filled with glue. I think the idea is to draw what it should have looked like."

The faint whiff of roll-ups and an overall worn too many months announced Alex's arrival. "Hello Miss Lawrenson. We don't get many visitors down this neck of the woods."

Alison greeted him with a smile. "James was just showing me his dove-tail. This is my form."

"Ah," Alex surveyed the third formers around them inquisitively. "Yours, eh? I haven't been giving them too many minus grades, have I?"

Alison tried not to sound frosty. "Actually, I don't remember your giving them any grades at all."

Alex looked confused. "I may have been ill that week." He looked around him again. "Nice lot, though. Chat about all sorts. One even knew who Tom Paxton was. Not Country Joe and the Fish, though." Alison let this go. Alex looked uncertain. "So, can I help you with anything?"

Alison wondered about asking if Tork was around, but decided against. "Just having a look at what they're up to, if that's okay?"

Alex shrugged. "Great. Nice of you to take an interest. I'm afraid they haven't really got on to any creative stuff for you to look at yet: just make a dove-tail joint then draw it as accurately as possible." It crossed Alison's mind that the sixth form syllabus Emily was following wasn't much different. Alex waved a hand at them. "But they'll show you: help yourself. Can I get you a coffee or anything?"

"No – no, thanks. I'll just..." she smiled and pointed at a workbench where three boys had taken out folders and were preparing to draw. Alex nodded encouragingly and went the other way.

Twenty minutes passed easily as her form showed her things and chatted away. Alex asked for everyone's attention and showed them something on the board once, but other than that the boys seemed content. Those who hadn't finished the making sought Alex's help, and those who'd started drawing made the task last by chattering quietly as they went.

Then the whole class leapt as one. An explosion - the magnified sound of a sail or canvas flicking full next door – whoomf - was followed by the clatter of landing debris. Alex and the class turned their faces to the noise but then the capacity for movement failed them. Gas explosion. A door behind burst open and Tork's slender figure wrestling with a fire extinguisher shot through the room and the next doorway to the explosion. Alison followed.

"Miles!" Tork had slowed down, but still held the extinguisher. Miles turned from the besmattered wall, all singed eyebrows and shock.

"I'm sorry, I'm sorry. I shouldn't have used that cheap valve, I'm sorry..."

Tork put the extinguisher down. "Are you alright?" Miles nodded. Tork surveyed the damage. "What were you doing?"

"Lighting methane. From sewage. I should have used a valve with a one way airlock, but I thought this one would be okay. I'm sorry."

Tork looked around. "Miles, you have literally covered us in shit." Miles looked at the floor. "And just to save on the cost of a valve? So when your father asks how your face got blown off I point out that he was the one who wanted you to save money?"

Miles looked uncomfortable. "It wasn't really so much about the cost. I'd have had to wait while we ordered one. And this one should have been..."

Tork had leapt forward and put his hand on the back of Miles' head, holding his eyes closely with his own. "Don't focus on why you did it. Focus on why you shouldn't have. You want to explain, to reassure yourself that you're not such an idiot. That you are still who you thought you were. But you *need* to be as shaken up as you feel now. You need to change into someone who will not take a risk like that again. Okay?" Miles stared back. Then nodded. Tork pulled him into a bear-hug, slapped his back, and released him again. "Alright?"

Miles nodded. "Alright." He paused. "Sir," he flicked a finger at Tork's front and then his own, "you're covered in shit now, sir."

Tork looked down and unbuttoned the overall. "It's what these are for." He turned and stooped for the extinguisher, surprised to realise he was being watched by Alison and some third formers. "Ah. Visitors. Just in time for the shit-show."

Alison smiled. The boys giggled and pointed at the ceiling.

"What?" Tork asked as he looked up.

"It's hit the fan, sir."

Alison offered to help with the clean-up, but Gareth soon arrived with gloves, disinfectant and all the proper kit, so they closed the room off and left him to it. Instead she helped Alex settle her form, pack them up and let them go slightly early for break, full of the news they would tell back at house.

"Coffee?" Alex asked. Alison hesitated.

"Aren't you going up for break?" she asked.

"We take it here. We have flapjack?"

Alison smiled, nodded and followed him into an office with a kettle.

The flapjack was excruciating. Alex apologised on his daughter's behalf. And the cup wasn't really clean, but the occasion was fine and the company interestingly different. Soon, Alison explained her difficulty with evening duties, and that Charles had suggested she ask for their help.

"Yes!" said Tork, with unexpected enthusiasm. "I can do that. Not that camera Charles remembers – I've got something better now. When can I come and do it?"

Alison didn't know. "Tomorrow?"

"Done. What time?"

"Whenever suits you…"

"When will you be there?"

"Gosh, er – lunchtime?"

"Okay. See you then."

"Great. Thank you so much." Alison sipped her coffee, just to recover a normal conversational pace. "Do either of you teach Emily?"

"Who?" Tork evidently didn't.

Alex replied. "Oh, Emily. No, she's Chris."

"Ah. Only she's absolutely amazing at fashion design, and pretty useless at mechanical engineering." Both looked at her without any obvious comprehension. "She seems to think that she could do something fashion-based for her A level?"

The phone rang and Alex got up to go and answer it. "Tork's the arty one," he said as he went.

Tork shrugged his shoulders. "I don't think there's any reason why not. Might be quite fun."

"So you could do it?"

Tork held his hands up. "Woah, there. Chris' pupil. And you'd have to get him to agree anyway – he's Head of Department."

Alison was surprised. "But Chris is a housemaster. They don't let you do both, do they?"

Tork looked amused. "Normally, maybe not. But Design teachers know the properties of their materials. And no-one is going to try and make a Head of Department out of me or Alex."

"Oh, come on – either of you would…"

Alison was cut off by Tork's raised finger, "We try to make this a bullshit-free zone."

She laughed. "Okay, I know what you mean. But you are full of surprises – Charles told me you revolutionised the CCF."

"Ha! 'CCF' and 'revolution' linked. Unusual."

"So what did you do?"

Tork shrugged. "Just taught Charles how street theatre works - blurring the line between the fiction and reality – keep them uncertain." He leaned forward. "Then further, unsettle not only the audience but the players…" He sat back again, and gave a low whistle. Alison didn't know if she needed to respond to this before trying to get back to Emily's fashion proposal. Period 4 soon. But she didn't get to decide anyway.

Alex came in. "It was for you." He sat down. Tork stood up. "But he's rung off now." Tork sat again. "I took a message." Tork spread his hands enquiringly. Alex took a bite of flapjack, rendering the message that bit harder to interpret. "Your friend on global health watch says there's one in China you'd like."

Tork stood up, looking excited. "Really?"

Alex looked up at him. "You're not going to disappear again, are you? Chris isn't here either."

Tork looked straight back. "Can you bring me in a decent newspaper tomorrow?" Alex nodded. Tork looked pleased for a second then disappointed. "But you won't remember!"

Alex nodded. "Good chance of that – but I will try." Tork looked unsatisfied.

Alison chipped in. "I'll get you one – a thank you for the camera." She didn't want him to forget his promise. Tork looked blankly at her for a second as if she were from some other dimension.

"Right, great. Probably *The Guardian* if you can manage it. Any broadsheet with decent international coverage."

She smiled and nodded. "Got it. See you lunchtime." She headed for the door. "Thanks for the coffee – and letting me come and see the lesson – and the flapjack."

Alex smiled. Tork was opening a cupboard. As she left the building and hurried back to the Maths block for period 4 the vision of Tork shooting past with his fire extinguisher, then giving Miles first a lecture then a hug, replayed in her head. He was pretty impressive, actually.

Into the woods

It was so much easier to cycle now that the fishing bag over his shoulder was empty, even on a rough track going uphill, and Tork enjoyed being able to appreciate the moonlight on the stately Corinthian arch as he approached it. He stopped when he got there, at least a mile from the nearest streetlight, probably from any kind of artificial light, and gazed up at the solid, grandiose architecture washed with the moon's spectral silver. He loved this estate. And anywhere in the middle of the night, when you had it to yourself, was a bit special. He imagined being a poacher, his wife and child asleep but hungry in the cottage in the woods, his game bag still empty, and a gamekeeper out there somewhere with a shotgun. Game on.

Abandoning the reverie but keeping the tone, he scanned the junction of paths that met at the arch and formed the original south entrance to the estate. The house itself was no longer accessible by vehicle from here, but there were lots of ways in by foot: the preferred route back from a taxi for furtive Bramblingums out at night. Gamekeeper now, Tork looked and listened for outlaws. Nothing.

Shoving the pedal and thus the bike back into action, Tork wobbled a revolution or two before wheeling into the darker space of the tree-lined avenue, the night sky disappearing above the canopy. A poor beam from his head-torch was his only guide through the potholes and loose stones on the downhill track as he descended to the locked, wrought-iron gates where the moonlight reappeared to silver-plate the view of the mansion in its commanding position above the lake. Tork pushed his bike round the outside of the gatepost and down a small, landscaped embankment on to a path. He paused and smiled at the eighteenth century before cycling off to the right and the woods on the eastern edge of the estate.

A tarmac tennis court appeared surreally far away from any other twentieth century addition to the grounds – an outpost of progress imposed on a landscape from another age – and then he crossed the palladian bridge and into the woods. Cycling was impossible here, even in the daytime, and Tork wavered between leaving his bike vaguely hidden in the trees, as usual, and pushing it home. He was tired, but he pushed it.

The moon shone sideways through narrow trunks here, and despite the awkward work of manoeuvring his bike, the slight complaint of his shoulders and legs, Tork felt alert and appreciative and alive to the magic of the moment. Walking on, looking around, soaking in the breathless summer night, a movement beyond the trees in the parkland caught his eye. He stopped and watched through the dark vertical lines spaced under the leaves, expecting, maybe, to spot Bramblingums up to no good. No, not bad guys. Badgers. He watched them as they snuffled in their exploratory fashion, seeking with their noses which bits of turf may be worth turning over with their powerful forepaws. Two of them, working their way up the hill. Then, suddenly and together, they stopped stock still, heads up. Had they caught his scent over this distance? But not even the air was moving. The moon marvelled along their white stripes for a moment, one snorted, and both moved on. Before Tork had finished watching them to the brow of the hill, he was startled by a cry and scuffle in the undergrowth deeper in the woods. For no good reason, he looked towards the sound, already ceased, then gently shook his head. "Love that!" he said quietly. Just life going on, almost unseen, around them.

There was no path but it was easy enough for him to find the lodge, even unlit as it was. He'd better get to bed – another late night tomorrow. He placed the bike gently against the fence, found his way through the gate, pushed the door open and stood in the tiny hallway listening to the breathing of his wife and child. Peering into the little box room, he saw Adds sleeping in the customised bed he'd built him into the corner. He made a tiny and pointless rearrangement to the bedding, then went and joined Eve in bed without waking her.

It begins

The next night saw Tork gazing over the same tranquil, sculpted, moonlit landscape south of the school, but this time from the roof. He'd done the work at Nelson House then just carried on fixing bits and pieces until he'd ended, last job, on his aerial on the mansion roof. All done. The yellow light from the windows of the building beneath him diminished as prefects switched off junior dormitories, and the aura around the house faded more quickly into the shining colourlessness of the grounds. Tork moved across to the north side where the boarding houses nestled in the colonnades and the courtyards behind them. Sixth form voices drifted through running taps and toothpasted mouths out of bathroom windows into the still night air. The settling process slowed, but continued. Lights that had gone off flicked on again briefly then, finally, went off for the night. At 10.40pm there was a mechanical click that made Tork turn to look behind him momentarily, but then he resumed his watch, a classical god on a frieze above an imperial portico, or perhaps a misplaced gargoyle strayed from a gothic temple.

It was shortly after eleven that a pair of headlights briefly illuminated the tree and cricket pavilion as they swung round towards the school. It parked considerately at the end of the colonnades and ejected Brick, who walked briskly to the door and into the house.

By eleven thirty Brick had ensured the summoning of all the housemasters despite the failure of the telephone system, and was engaged in earnest chat with the Head as the housemasters gathered next door in Elizabeth's office.

Roger, in the nearest house, arrived last. "What's up, chaps?" he greeted his fellows.

John never missed an opportunity to be one up on Roger. "Didn't you see the news?"

"The news?" Roger had assumed some minor crisis of disappearing or partying or drug-taking Bramblingums, not something off the national news.

Dominic hadn't seen it either. "The late news? What channel was it on?"

Tony muttered. "I prefer the radio, but lost reception altogether about 10.30. Odd, because reception's usually better at night."

This caught Michael's interest. "Is it? I get more interference at night."

Tony replied wisely, "Yes, that's *because* reception is better: you pick up all sorts of other things besides the channel you want. But tonight it just went dead."

Michael looked wistful. "Ah, picking up all sorts of things at night: those were the days."

Simon, uncharacteristically, made himself heard, "But what was it on the news?" and managed to get them to the point. But at that moment Brick opened the door and ushered them into the Head's presence. No Elizabeth, of course. So no coffee. Now that the cashmere turtleneck season was over and they were deep into the summer of loose-fitting low-buttoned silk blouses, Elizabeth leaning over in front of them to offer her tray of coffee cups was the highlight of any meeting for several of the housemasters. Some even took sugar in the summer only. Still, at least this meeting promised some drama.

Each went to his normal seat, some having to move the furniture around to achieve the normal arrangement. They quietened expectantly.

"Shall I take minutes in Elizabeth's absence, Headmaster?"

Whitley nodded. "Thank you, Ian." He watched Brick take out a wad of file paper and balance it on his knee. "You'll know as much as I do: the television appeared to stop working soon after 10.30, and then we had this news bulletin. BBC format, but it appeared on all three channels. An unfamiliar newsreader ran through this item about some sort of disease having arrived from China via Hong Kong, to which we're all particularly susceptible, apparently. Everyone is to stay home until further notice. Then the normal tv close-down, but a bit early. And whether or not it's a coincidence, the phones are down. And that's where we are."

The information was absorbed silently by some, recycled thoughtfully by others, for a moment or two. A thought occurred to Chris. "Will our Hong Kong boys already have it, do you think?"

John was the biologist. "They'll have flown over, what, about two weeks ago now? Depends on the disease – whether it's viral or not and so on – but probably not, I'd say. Possible, though."

"Do we isolate them?"

John shrugged. Roger intervened. "I think we'd need a pretty solid case before we did that. Parents aren't going to like a knee-jerk reaction against the overseas community."

"This may be more serious than PR." Simon was surprising everyone tonight. Eyes drifted to the Head to take the lead. He cleared his throat.

"We need the bursar, really. Did you call him, Ian?"

Brick looked worried. "I just went straight to housemasters..."

"And Deborah?"

Brick looked alarmed. "Deborah! Sorry – forgot. I'll go round there straight afterwards."

The Head turned, obviously about to say he'd give them a ring, then remembered himself and faced the circle again. "I'm assuming that none of the boys – or girls," he added, careful not to make the same mistake as Brick had, "knows anything of this yet?" They all shook heads, although each was conscious that someone could easily have been still in the house television room ten minutes after they should theoretically have left it. "We'll work on that assumption. So our first move will be to have house assemblies first thing in the morning in order to tell them whatever we're going to tell them."

Lots of nods. So far, so easy. Simon spoke. "Unless you want to have a school assembly in chapel and address them yourself?"

Confusion. Brick looked up from his notes. "It would certainly ensure consistency of message." And it would mean that Brick wouldn't miss anything.

John and Roger instinctively reacted against Brick's centralisation of everything. "It's a very personal and potentially upsetting thing. The boys will be worried about their parents – I think we'll need to meet in house…"

"We could maybe follow up with a school assembly, but definitely start with house…"

"It's easy to have a house assembly before breakfast, whereas a school one…"

Dominic chipped in. "Will there be any breakfast? How many of the catering staff live in?"

Tony decided to support Brick. "It wouldn't be hard to organise a school assembly first thing, then maybe we could follow up after whatever sort of breakfast is possible? It would be good to have a clear, universal message then the smaller, house meetings to tease through the details."

Simon interrupted. "Perhaps we should work out what we're actually going to do before debating how to communicate it." Really, as the most recently appointed housemaster he did seem to be rather getting above himself and becoming almost critical. Crises take people in peculiar ways. Anyway, who actually started this debate?

The Head tried to make progress. "We need to keep a normal routine going as far as is possible. Let's just go through the day and see what will work as normal, and what won't."

Brick had one of his occasional moments of incisiveness. "Lessons and activities should be manageable; it's eating that's going to be the problem." A ripple of alarm went around the room as the truth of this sunk in.

"Gosh, yes," someone murmured.

They looked hopefully at the Head. He ducked it. "Well, putting that aside for a minute, we think we can run a normal-enough programme for a few days? We can manage without those staff who live off campus?" No-one present was even vaguely involved with the timetable or cover, but they were happy to reassure the Head that this should be possible. And Lionel would manage activities. "So we're okay until the food runs out."

Sober nods. Roger speculated. "Perhaps the boys could help boost the ranks of the catering staff? And the CCF have compo rations. D of E boys are used to cooking for themselves. The community service boys who can't go off campus could go to the kitchens instead. And the girls, of course."

Deborah wasn't there to echo "of course" ironically. No-one else thought of it.

"Okay," said the Head. "And we need a way of ensuring that we get any new information as soon as possible. Perhaps we can leave a television permanently on in Elizabeth's room, then we'll know that whatever is broadcast, someone reliable will have taken notes."

"But Elizabeth won't be here," Tony gasped. A flutter of anxiety in the room reflected the general feeling that it was actually Elizabeth who kept things going at Brambling. How would any of them manage the Head without her?

The Head looked up. "No, she's here. She'll be in in the morning as usual."

"Here?" Tony asked. "She hasn't gone home?"

"Not tonight, as it happens. Lucky break: she worked late. Staying with Deborah and Philip now, I believe." He glanced quickly at Brick. "Could have had all three of them here had we remembered."

Brick looked embarrassed. Everyone else looked intrigued. Working late, with Whitley, presumably, but then going on to Deborah's.

Speculation was interrupted by a knock on the door. Everyone expected to see Elizabeth, Deborah and Philip, somehow, but it was Tork.

Tork?

The Head was the first to express it aloud. "Tork?"

Tork nodded and moved forward so he was sort of part of the circle. He had a large board with him which he placed at his feet, resting against his legs. "Sorry to interrupt, and I know I haven't got an Oxbridge degree in Classics or anything, but I thought you might want to hear what I have to say anyway because I actually was living in a Kibbutz when a particularly nasty flu variant swept the country killing people. We sealed ourselves in, it passed over and round us, and we emerged into the aftermath unscathed. So I think I know what we have to do to get through this. Also, I'm from the CDT department, and I can make things." He turned his board round. It had "No Entry. Disease Control" written on it.

The Head seemed genuinely interested. "Go on."

Tork indicated the board. "People will come. As soon as things get rough out there, they'll see this as a possible safe haven and arrive at the gates. Relatives of people here will come. You have to turn them away. Get the CCF, full cammo gear and rifles, with these signs and a barricade at the gates, daybreak. Use one of Steve's trailers and some coils of barbed wire."

"Barbed wire?" Dominic was shocked.

Tork turned on him. "It has to look the part, okay? People associate rolls of barbed wire and soldiers with Ulster, serious security, high stakes."

"Soldiers?" Michael also seemed uncertain.

"The CCF look intimidating enough if you don't know them. And young soldiers are scarier – they're inexperienced and nervous, more likely to shoot. If anyone does get heavy, Charles or someone will be there with them to step in. Good if we can find some surgical masks for them."

"Will the boys be alright doing this?" Michael was still unsure.

"They'll love it. It'll be like another of their exercises, except better. Like a play that goes a bit real for a moment." No-one could see anything else wrong with any of this. Tork pressed on. "The gate's fine for the first day or two, but we should use Sunday for a full-school operation making as much of a perimeter as possible secure, even against walkers. We'll need to set patrols. We'll also need lots and lots of help on the farm and in the kitchens."

"The farm!" The Head looked pleased. "Can it feed us?"

Tork pulled a face. "Nowhere near, but we need to start it going in that direction, and the boys need to see that we've got a plan, and everyone needs apparently important activity. If we commandeer the cows in the outer park then we've got the promise of milk and cheese, anyway."

The Head nodded. "Yes, yes." Everyone else nodded. "Chris, get Tork a chair, will you?"

There wasn't really room in the circle for another chair, and Chris put the one he fetched from Elizabeth's room a little into the middle. Tork sat with the circle around him.

"What else?" the Head asked him.

Part Two

James on the run

Not yet seven o'clock in the morning, but already it was warm, especially if you were running. James panted and sweated. But that was okay: seeing as his punishment run was unsupervised, he needed a bit of sweat and breathlessness in case anyone checked up on him when he returned. He was on no particular route, exploring some parts of the estate he had never seen yet.

Being out in the Brambling parkland on another glorious summer morning didn't trouble James, but this szlachta thing that had got him there was on his mind. Mr Parker had asked why the Design staff had been discussing the Polish/Lithuanian aristocracy, James had admitted that they hadn't, and Mr Parker had retorted that he had to define the word *in its context.* He'd made a big deal of it: apparently it was a crucial comprehension technique. But the context wasn't easy to remember with any precision, and what he could recall didn't fit with the snippets he'd found from dictionaries and encyclopaedias and teachers. And then his visit to the library after prep meant that he'd missed his cookroom duty and Josh hadn't been able to cover it after all and the house prefect thought that being late for lights-out because you were doing your cookroom duty late was *two* offences, and James had decided not to risk arguing, in case that would have made it three. It may have been the darkness of injustice and ignorance – he still didn't know how to define szlachta in his next English lesson – brooding just below the blue sky and deepening colours created by the climbing sun that made him swerve away from the little path entering the woods from the palladian bridge. But the main track leading directly back to school looked dusty and harsh, so he compromised and ran up a trail of flattened grass at the side of the woodland, just far enough from the trees to be still in the sun, where early butterflies were taking to the air.

Almost immediately he had to stop: whether it was the sun flickering through the tops of the trees, the difference between the bright grass and shadowed woodland, the flutter of cabbage white wings, or a bit of exhaustion or what, having an hallucination was pretty unnerving. He peered through the trees again, trying to let his eyes adjust to the dimmer light. Suddenly, slipping in and out of view between the trees, there they were: a lady and a little boy, walking slowly through the woods, naked. His mouth fell open. They were there. And they were naked.

Insect life stopped and grass and tree limbs stood still. They were just past him now, drifting down the hill, shadows sliding over the bodies and dappling their skin as the narrow tree trunks continued their slow procession past them. The boy held something up in his little hand, and she crouched for a second to look at it with him. They seemed to have grasses or wildflowers in their hair. He must have dropped his find, because when she straightened and they walked on, he was holding her hand instead. James, dead still, watched them go. He had a dim awareness that if he had been with others then his and their ribaldry and lewd appreciations would have drowned everything else out. But he was alone and it was all that stuff that was drowned out by his awe at having slipped into a classical idyll and seen a goddess, off duty, relaxed, at play, magical. It was a vision, and he was already turning himself into a tree, rooted, gazing at the leafy spot where they had disappeared. He felt elated, privileged, a participator in something beautiful. Then his eyes misted slightly as a wave of something sadder swept over him. He didn't recognise it at first. When he did, he was confused by it: he really missed his mum.

Blinking back tears, it occurred to him that he was sufficiently alone to cry if he wanted to, but the reflex to push it away was too strong. And then he noticed the movement to his right, out of the trees on the edge of the strong light. They were coming straight at him, up the same trail, their flesh now fully lit. He was going to be caught spying on them. And crying. It never occurred to him as the remotest possibility to act naturally and say hello. Twisting to run away in panic, he stumbled, failed to save himself, and fell awkwardly, glancing off a low, broken branch before landing face down. In the moment it took him to gather himself, he knew he'd missed his chance to flee.

"Are you alright?" Eve asked as she and Adds approached. "Have you hurt yourself? That looked a nasty fall."

James lifted his face from the ground, but didn't really like to look. "I'm okay, I think, thanks. I caught my foot." There was an odd stinging gathering and flaring on his right shoulder. He raised himself on to his elbow and his left hand went instinctively to the sensation, and as instinctively drew sharply back from the touch.

"Have you cut your shoulder? Let's see." She rolled his t-shirt up, exposing his back and, higher up, a raw graze with a bit of a bloody hole in it. "Yes, there's a bit of a puncture and a graze. Let's slip this shirt over your head." Being undressed by a naked lady was too odd. James just complied with the minimum movement and kept watching the ground in front of him. "It's not too bad. We'd better clean it and put a bit of a dressing on, though. We're just nearby – can you get up okay?"

"Yes, I'm fine, I think." James stood and, with an effort, turned to face her.

She smiled. "This is Adds." She looked down at him and patted his little shoulder.

"Hello." James nodded.

"And I'm Eve – Mrs Fry, I should say, I suppose." James nodded a greeting helplessly. "Oh," Eve sensed the problem, "um...", she looked around her for a second then held up his shirt, "would you like me to put this on? Sorry, I forget how embarrassed people get – I lived with naturists once – you'd probably prefer I covered up?" This was an impossible question and James managed no coherent reply. "May I borrow your t-shirt?"

This was a much easier one. "Yes, of course."

In her new white dress Eve led them both back to the cottage. James walked with his left hand over his right shoulder, holding his finger where Eve had placed it to put a little pressure on the wound. The sharp pain was okay, but the graze around it raged a bit.

"Were you training for sports day or something?" Eve asked.

"No – more of a punishment run."

"Oh?"

It was too much to explain. "I forgot to clean the cookroom."

"Gosh," Eve smiled, "I'd be running every day all summer! We'd better not let you see our kitchen when we get in, had we, Adds?" Adds looked up but ignored the question as being beyond comprehension.

James wasn't sure how exactly to respond either, but wanted to say something. "Is it short for Adam, his name?"

Eve laughed lightly. "Well, his name is actually Dylan, but we started calling him Adam as a bit of a joke." James looked uncertain. "My name's Eve... and we live in a sort of paradise? Would you Adam and Eve it?" James acknowledged the joke at last. "And then it sort of stuck. So Adds it is, most of the time."

They walked through the grasses a little further, the seeds and lazy midges catching half-heartedly at their bare legs, before turning on to a track that ran from the Gothic Temple into the woods. Then Eve turned right again on to a soft grassy avenue leading to the cottage.

James paused. "I've never been here."

Eve looked over her shoulder and paused. "No. Hardly anyone comes even as far as the Gothic Temple usually."

James pointed further down the track they were turning off. "What's that way?"

Eve gazed through the trees in that direction. "An old gateway on to farm land. It must have been used by someone as access to the estate once. Or possibly a way off it for hunters and horses, I don't know. It's chained shut now." She indicated the cottage. "This will have been a little gate lodge. But it's our home now. Come on, let's get you patched up and back to school."

She found him a chair in the sitting room where Adds showed him a painted wooden cow until she returned, some shorts and a shirt on now, with a bowl of clean water and some dressings and antiseptic. She gently cleaned the little wound and then applied a dressing – one a bit too big, really, but it kept the sticking plaster off the worst of the graze.

"All done." She walked round in front of him.

"Thank you," he looked unthinkingly for his shirt.

"Oh, your shirt – I left it next door." She hesitated. "I'll wash it for you, shall I?"

"No, no – it's fine, really."

"Sure? It's no trouble..."

James was a little flustered. "No, thanks, Miss – I need it to go back in."

"Okay. But I put the kettle on – would you like a cup of tea before you go back?"

"Oh, er..."

She put her head on one side and nodded encouragingly. "I would – good for the shock, you know. Plenty of sugar in a nice milky cup of tea. Not too hot, so you can drink it quickly and not be late."

James smiled. "Okay, thanks, Miss."

She laughed. "I don't think I could get used to being called 'Miss'," she said, as she left the room.

Adds ran off into the garden and James listened to Eve rattling things in the kitchen. Maybe he should go and help or something, but she had said he wasn't to see the kitchen. He decided to wait to be waited upon.

Two cups in hand, Eve appeared in the tiny hall, but was looking out into the garden. Then she turned her head towards James. "Shall we sit on the step? There's a little sun here coming through the trees – and I can watch Adam."

"Okay." She stepped out and sat on the step to one side, placing the two cups of tea on the paving stone in front, and James sat next to her. He would have put on his shirt, but she seemed to have forgotten to get it, and the sun was nice on his skin. He didn't like to ask again, and couldn't go and look for it, so sat without it.

Eve watched Adam encouraging his wooden cow to do some grazing on the shaggy lawn. "He can do this for hours." They watched him together in comfortable silence. "We're a bit ahead of our usual schedule today: Tork – Mr Fry – was a bit restless and off to school very early. He must have something on. Adds woke early." James thought about the fact that this was Mr Fry's family.

"Miss?"

She allowed herself a half giggle at the term. "Yes?"

"I don't suppose you know what a szlachta is, do you?"

She turned to him with some surprise. "Well, yes. I do."

"Only, I know it's something to do with the polish aristocracy. But I think it's also something to do with..." James furrowed his brow, "I don't know... the way things are... sort of... organised, I think."

She nodded. "That's right. The szlachta were indeed the aristocracy in the lands either side of the Polish/Lithuanian border from about the sixteenth century, and it's amazing really that about a hundred years before the civil war in this country..." She glanced at her audience and checked herself. "Anyway, the thing you mention is probably because they were allodial not feudal, which means they were landowners – really proper landowners." James looked anxious. She shouldn't have used those terms, and needed a re-start. "You know about William the Conqueror?"

James nodded. "Battle of Hastings. He shot Harold in the eye with an arrow."

"Well..." Eve checked herself again and decided to leave explaining the Bayeux tapestry for another time. "...that's the one, yes. Well after that, he decreed that all the land in England belonged to him, you see. All his. Only he couldn't live in all of it, so he lent bits of it to his friends and nobles to farm and build castles and manors in. But in return for the favour, he often required them to do things for him, like collect taxes and raise armies or fight."

"Like rent?" James asked.

She seemed pleased. "Exactly. So landowners here didn't really own it at all. They had it as long as the King allowed them to, and they could only pass it on to their families if he agreed." James nodded. "They acted as if they were in charge in their estates, and would have been really bossy and unpleasant to the ordinary people who worked there, but they actually had one eye on the king and what he wanted the whole time, and never forgot they were just a little part of a bigger estate."

James was getting the idea. "But the szlachta..." She nodded encouragingly at him. "They *did* own their land?"

"That's right."

"And ran things how they wanted?"

"Pretty much."

James absorbed the idea. "So no rules, really, except what they decided was necessary in their own estate?"

She beamed. "Very good – that's exactly what makes them so interesting to study."

"They live in a sort of world of their own."

Eve braked a bit. "Well, sort of, I suppose – maybe that's overdoing it a bit..."

James shrugged apologetically. "It's just something my mum says to me sometimes." He drank his tea. He thought he knew now what to say in English. What a bit of luck.

Soon after, Eve took the cups in and brought out his shirt. James said his thanks and ran off. He got back up to the Gothic Temple track and headed for school and breakfast, but was surprised to see a land rover on its way towards him. He stood aside and let it pass. It had several older boys in full CCF uniform in the back, and it was headed straight for the gap in the woods by Eve's house. James was really pleased that Eve was dressed now.

Charles on guard

At the main gate, Charles checked his watch: 11.30am. Camp coffee was alright out in the wilds, but a bit disappointing just a mile away from the common room at break time. He wondered about letting the boys urinate in the trees: there were staff houses and families just the other side. On the other hand, they could hardly walk a mile back to school, so would the householders rather have boys weeing in the bushes or knocking on the door asking to use the bathroom? The proper military answer would be to dig a latrine. Maybe they'd have to do that if this was to go on. Or Dave the common room steward would have to move out of the little lodge that was part of the gate structure so that they could take it over as a command post.

He stifled a bit of a yawn. It was actually past lunch time if you took into consideration the rather surprisingly early start Wilko had sprung on him. He hadn't seen the news the previous night, so having Wilko, or CO Rev. Major Wilkinson (reserves), Bramblingum CCF, banging on the door and barging into his flat at 4.30am had been quite a surprise. And then it had just got more surreal from there. And by 06hundred hours he'd mustered a few troops and was watching Steve the Groundsman manoeuvre a big, ugly, heavy trailer across the classical grade one listed gateway. They unlocked the pedestrian gate, helped arrange rolls of barbed wire around, then Tork had appeared briefly with protective masks for them, and they'd spread out across the road to challenge approaching vehicles. He'd been a bit apprehensive at first. The boys hadn't seemed especially perturbed by the news, and reacted instead to the novelty of being roused from their beds, issued with rifles, and swept off to guard the gates against all comers. But maybe having to turn people away – off-campus staff, delivery drivers, maybe parents or keen visitors of landscaped gardens and classical mansions – and possibly even having to explain to them what was going on – maybe this would cause the news of national catastrophe to sink in and worry them.

But actually hardly anyone had come. One or two colleagues had turned in as if to approach, seen the "Disease Control" sign and, as if having confirmed something they needed to know, waved at Charles and turned around. Quite a few cars drove along the road, sometimes giving the military presence on the turn-off into the school a curious look as they passed, but hardly anyone had actually driven up to the gates all morning. The boys were surprisingly normal; perhaps they thought it was just another impromptu exercise that got them out of the classroom and into cammo gear in the sun, so best not to question it. Well, housemasters could sort that out later.

Then a smooth-looking Jaguar of some kind was indicating and slowing on the road. The boys nearest the junction squared their shoulders into a more military stance, brought their rifles forward off their shoulders but still pointing at the sky, and took a step forward, challenging. Charles watched them appreciatively: excellent. The car turned off the road towards them then stopped and wound a window down. A well-groomed head appeared. Parent, probably.

One of the guards spoke first. "Sorry, sir – I can't approach. Please turn your car around, sir."

The head nodded understandingly and a hand appeared and pointed behind them at Charles. "Can I have a word with your commanding officer over there?"

The boys wavered and glanced behind at Charles. He nodded and walked forward until he was just, but only just, in front of his soldiers. "I'm sorry, sir, I must ask you to keep your distance."

The man nodded understandingly. "That's alright, I quite understand. I just need to leave something for Robert Johnson of Talbot House. He needs it before the weekend. Can you get it to him for me, please?" He opened the door.

"Stay in your car, please, sir."

Mr Johnson senior looked irritated but long-suffering. He shut the door, produced a package from the car seat next to him and held it out of the window. "Okay," he seemed to wink a little, "can you just take it, then?"

Charles peered at him. "It may be contaminated." Mr Johnson's expression was changing to 'enough of this nonsense I'm a busy man' so Charles decided to compromise. "You can put it on the ground there. I'll see he gets it before the weekend."

Mr Johnson guided it to the ground by his car. "Okay, Officer – thank you." He was smiling condescendingly and shaking his head a little as he reversed and drove off.

Charles caught the eye of his nearest cadet and made a face.

"What shall we do with it, sir?"

"Just leave it for the moment. We'll maybe disinfect it or find out a little more about the way this disease is transmitted before bringing it in or touching it. It's alright there."

The boy had a look at it, decided he couldn't tell what it was, and lost interest. Charles gazed after the car. Odd reaction, really, but there was no knowing what people did and didn't know, or what was going on out there. He was maybe the sort of Brambling parent who thought all politicians were scaremongering shysters playing games of their own and to be ignored as long as possible. And that if they were serious about him staying at home and stopping his business activities, then they'd slap him with a fine sooner or later and they could take it from there.

A blackbird called from the tree-lined avenue inside the gates and a slight breeze fluttered the leaves and made Charles think of sailing. He closed his eyes a second. It was nice to stop.

"Sir?" He opened them again and looked enquiringly at Lance-Corporal Tom Winters. "Car coming, sir." Charles looked at the road junction blankly. "No, sir – from school."

Charles turned and was deeply surprised by a little lurch of pleasure: it was Alison's car.

The mini descended the hill to the humpback bridge over the water, bobbled over it and pulled up the ascent to the gateway. It wavered as it approached: Alison was obviously going to pull off the road on to the grass to park, then realised the road was a dead-end anyway, so she just stopped still on it. Charles smiled, raising his hand in an awkward little wave, and started walking back to the pedestrian gate as Alison emerged from the car and surveyed the trailer with its barbed-wire topping in front of her. She gestured at it while looking through it at Charles approaching.

"Expecting them to storm the barricades on foot?"

Charles inspected it. "It *is* a bit much, isn't it? I gather Tork thought that a trailer looked like a temporary obstacle, whereas a trailer with this on top is a deliberate barrier."

"Tork?" Alison was surprised. "What's he got to do with it?"

Charles shrugged. "I really don't know. Apparently his 'input has been useful' quote unquote the Reverend Major Brian Wilkinson (Reserves) Company Commander, Brambling College CCF."

"Ah. Praise indeed." Alison tucked her hair behind her ear, although it was too short to require this adjustment.

"You weren't hoping to get through?" Charles was concerned.

"No," she said, "no, no – I brought you coffee. Bill said he'd been asked to cover your lessons all morning, and we both knew you'd be struggling without real coffee. I've got some in a flask."

Charles beamed. "Well, how very kind and thoughtful – thank you."

"Oh," she swatted it away, "you know – and I was interested to see your operation up here."

Charles turned to the boys watching them and suddenly barked. "Squad! A-ten-*shun*! Inspecting Officer present!" He went to the pedestrian gate and opened it as the boys faced the front and stamped their feet.

Alison skipped through the gate. "Oh! I wasn't expecting that. What do I do?"

Charles was also at attention. "Just like you've seen in the movies, ma'am."

Charles in attendance, Alison walked in front of the two rows of boys, three of them near the gate and two a little closer to the road. She looked the first two up and down, nodded. Went to the third. "Where you from, soldier?"

"Ma'am! Chipping Norton, Ma'am."

Alison raised her eyebrows. "Nice. You like being in the army?"

"Ma'am, yes, ma'am."

Alison turned. She was behind one of the other two boys. She tapped him on the shoulder. "Show me the sole of your left boot." He picked the foot up. She had no idea what she was looking for. "Okay – at ease." A flicker of uncertainty shivered through the five at-attention boys. "Sorry – I just meant you can put your boot down." She glanced at Charles and gave an "oops screwed up" face, but Charles remained stony. She recovered and continued. Then she seemed to have finished, really. "Very good, er..." she had no idea what rank Charles was.

"Captain, ma'am."

"Captain, of course. Very good, Captain. Well done, everybody." She walked back to the gate.

"Squad, at ease!" A co-ordinated movement. "And easy – but still on duty. Take over, Lance-Corporal." Charles concluded, and followed Alison.

Alison turned just through the gate. "Sorry – made a mess of it..."

Charles smiled. "You were excellent – although I think they *did* suspect you weren't some high-ranking General at all."

She reached into the car and handed him a flask and mug. "How are they taking it all?"

Charles automatically glanced over his shoulder at the boys. "They seem fine, I think. I don't know if they really know whether or not to take it seriously yet." He took the coffee off her. "This is great, thanks."

She dipped back into the car. "Shortbread?"

Charles's eyes widened. "You are an angel!"

"Shouldn't you share it with your men?"

He looked horrified. "Certainly not. Are you mad?"

They laughed. The young trees breathed a ripple of applause through their leaves.

"How about you? How are you dealing with it?"

Charles wasn't sure how personally to field this. Surely not to discuss concerns about his parents, brother, friends outside the school... He hesitated. "Oh, same as them, really. Haven't really processed anything yet. I mean Sergeant Wilko kind of "briefed" me, Steve said this was a rum one, a guy in a car winked like it was all baloney, and if I think about it I'm all questions and no information, so best to just get on with it. Follow orders. Ours not to reason why. Have you heard anything more?"

Alison watched him pour the coffee. "No. No-one seems to know anything, really. People have been checking the phones, their tvs and radios, but no-one seems to have got anything. The house assemblies seemed deliberately abrupt – just that this has happened, we don't know more yet, tell you later and meanwhile business as usual. Some of the girls were really spooked, and of course we've no idea what's happened to the day girls, so we're worrying about them."

Charles nodded. "Of course. We have so few day boys that we tend to forget about that."

Alison gazed beyond him at the boys standing on guard. "There are quite a few missing from classes. Some of the CCF boys, of course, day girls and boys, then some have been selected by housemasters to go to the farm – with Tork, I suppose – and some have gone to the kitchens with Geoff and with Greg, apparently."

"Greg?"

Alison nodded. "Apparently well known for his baking skills. That homemade food shop in Artle takes everything he and his wife make, so the story goes, and keeps asking them for more. Whenever things get a bit much – so quite often – apparently he always says he'll chuck in the teaching and just bake."

"Really? Full of surprises, our Languages department, I always say. Although it doesn't sound very French, does it? Greg's custard tarts..."

"Greg's bread buns..."

"Greg's sausage rolls...

"Greg's stotty cake..."

Charles did a double-take. "Greg's what?"

Alison waved a hand. "Sorry – it's a northern thing."

"Ah," Charles nodded knowingly, "yes, the north. I went there once."

Alison looked interested. "Really?"

"Yes – near Scotland, isn't it?"

But Alison changed course. "I wonder how they're dealing with all this." She looked back down the drive.

Charles sensed the change. "Is that where you have family?"

She nodded. "My parents, yes. And a little sister still at uni."

"They'll be okay, I expect. Like us – stay home and wait it out." Alison nodded unconvinced and said nothing. It half-occurred to

Charles to squeeze her hand or touch her shoulder, but before the thought had formed he'd already gone for lightening the mood again. "And students are invulnerable. Your sister will be drinking herself immune."

Alison attempted a laugh. "Probably." She looked around. "Oh, I meant to say - Tork did those cameras – did I tell you? They're brilliant, I think. I haven't tried to get a photo off one yet, but I've got this little box in my room with a screen on it so you can tell it's working when you turn it on, and he says if I unplug the box and take it down to the workshops the next morning he should be able to get a photo of something that happened the night before. Pretty cool, huh?"

"Very cool." Charles didn't risk using that sort of word without a sardonic twist in his voice. It didn't really belong in his vocabulary.

"So thanks for the nod – much appreciated."

Charles mock-bowed. "Glad to be of service."

She smiled and nodded. "Anyway, I'd best get back – lessons to teach, you know…"

"Ah, yes," Charles considered. "I wonder what on earth Bill will be setting for mine."

"Something creating lots of marking, I expect…"

Charles's eyes bulged. "Well he can do it himself if so, thank you very much!" He made to drink up his coffee.

Alison stopped him. "Oh, take your time over that. Don't worry about the cup and flask – you can return them anytime." She waved her fingers and got back into the car. Charles watched her start the engine, reverse and turn. He raised his mug to her just as she looked back before driving off, then watched the mini as it fell, bobbed over the bridge, and climbed again. Then he took his coffee back through the side gate and readied himself for another hour or more on guard duty.

Tom looked across at the coffee. "Is Miss your girlfriend, sir?"

Charles looked knowing. "I couldn't possibly comment on the private lives of staff and officers to underlings such as yourself – you know that."

"Ah," said Tom, "but as a member of the editorial team and a journalist of *The Rag,* sir, I have a right to ask what's in the public interest."

Charles liked a bit of a debate, and was also a history teacher, after all. "Public interest? Define your terms there, reporter."

"I notice you're avoiding the original question, sir. Can I take that as confirmation?"

"I notice you're avoiding defining your terms, boy. Can I take that as confirmation you don't know what you're talking about?"

Tom paused, sighed and struggled. "Well, in the interest of the public. Our readership would be interested to know…" Charles covered his face with a hand as a gesture of despair in the stupidity of his opposition. "Okay, okay, sir, don't panic. I know that isn't really what public interest is, although we are a bit of a scurrilous gossip-mongering rag – your words, sir – so it is part of our brief. But…"

There was a pause. Charles raised an eyebrow. "Go on, then, Tom. This is the bit where you show that there actually is a legitimate public interest in any possible romantic entanglements on the staff apart from filling your infamously inaccurate 'rumours' feature?"

"Um – corruption, sir. A free press guards against corruption."

Charles looked mock-impressed with this idea. "Of course. And the possibilities for corruption here are… hmm?"

Tom was still scrabbling around, but then he got something. "Ah – okay. Suppose Miss Lawrenson were to punish me unjustly…"

"Ridiculously hypothetical, but go on."

"And suppose," Tom adopted an ah-ha tone, "I were in *your* form, sir? Shouldn't I have the right to know before going to my form-master with a concern about my maths teacher that my form-master has, you know, *an interest* in my maths teacher?"

Charles, caught, nodded. "Okay: neat. Fortunately staff professionalism at this school is beyond reproach, of course."

"Oh, of *course*," Tom replied with just enough sarcasm. "But there are no codes of conduct against relationships between staff?"

"No."

"Just against admitting it?"

"*Or* denying it..."

"Ah!" Tom jumped up and down. "So you won't deny it!"

Charles turned his face away with a smile. "Of course not – no comment on..."

"Rumours of an unmilitary liaison are not denied..."

"You wouldn't dare – and you wouldn't spell 'liaison' correctly."

"If I check first, can I write it?"

Charles hadn't expected to be asked permission. "It's not about imposing censorship – it's about you taking responsibility for the truthfulness of what you write."

"It's only a rumour, sir."

"Is it?"

"Well, it will be once I've published it." Charles hesitated. Perhaps he should ask him not to publish it. "Respect to you, sir – she's got great legs."

Now Charles was really uneasy. "Okay, you've crossed a line there, Lance-Corporal. Back to your post."

"Yes, sir, sorry, sir," with or without irony, it was impossible to tell, Tom came to attention, saluted, did an about-turn and watched the road. Charles looked at his back. A year ago, Tom had been a real smart-alec and would have responded to the minor humiliation of being checked by pushing harder, trying to show he wasn't wrong really. But he'd handled himself well today: clever, but backed off quickly when he overstepped the mark. He was growing up.

He wasn't so sure about his own performance, though. Had he just converted Alison's kindly gesture into a salacious rumour? Would *The Rag* print something, and how would Alison feel about it? Around the grit of this concern arose the pearly glow of their mutual involvement in this atmosphere of expectation. Perhaps if the whole idea was so credible, so popular, then a rumour could become something more.

Tork on the range

Tork tipped his imaginary cowboy hat back a little with his thumbnail on his forehead, drew on his cigarette, and crossed his hands on the horn of his saddle in Marlborough man pose. Bramblingums were amazing – especially, perhaps, the country ones. Ask the housemasters for a handful of boys who could ride, or could take down half a flock of geese with shotguns, or use a ferret to catch rabbits, and they always came up trumps. A posse had been very easy to assemble. And here they were, rustling cattle with him.

Paul turned off the engine of the three-wheeler and the sudden silence drew Tork's attention. He looked down to Paul on the little all-terrain vehicle they'd got from the grounds team. "Needs a fourth wheel, really."

Paul patted his vehicle. "Alright with three."

Tork nodded. "But nice and slow on the cornering – okay?"

"Nice and slow." Paul nodded fervently. In truth, he never wanted anything to go fast anyway. Tork was actually a little envious of the bike: he didn't really know how to ride his horse. His being on a pony far too small for him was partly to give the best riders the bigger ones, but mainly to let him have a safer seat. He and Paul watched from the crest of the hill while the boys rode confidently down the side of the field to circle around below the cattle in the sunshine.

Tork looked out beyond the first field to the ones below, then the occasional house and the hints of building masked by trees showing where the nearest village was. All peaceful on a glorious morning. No sign of a vicious epidemic raging, but then there wouldn't be, unless maybe a blue-flashing ambulance siren might come to split the peace of the hibernation. Then with so little traffic, would it use all that anyway? Or would it skulk in quietly beneath the radar to take away another casualty?

The boys had reached the bottom of the field and were spreading out along the bottom fence. They settled, then the wide ones moved out a bit wider, controlling the horses expertly. There was a pause while they looked at each other, then Ben in the middle held his hand aloft. Tork signalled back – ready. As one, the three riders waved their arms wildly and their voices came up the hill, "Yip! Yip! Gid'up, there!" One or two of the cows began to move cautiously up the hill away from them. "Yip!" The horses wheeled around a little as the boys carried on shouting. Tork and Paul looked at each other, eyes shining.

"Yeee-ha!" said Tork.

"Yee-ha!" replied Paul, and waved his sun hat.

One cow mooed. Several were walking now, and one even stumbled momentarily into a near run. They were easing up the hill, and the horses and riders were beginning to shift their positions to escort them.

"Better go." Tork pulled on the reins, hoping his horse would turn and head back, and Paul fired up the bike which, fortunately, didn't seem to worry Tork's steed one bit. It shambled round and headed for the gate at a leisurely walk. Paul finished his turn and soon overtook, heading to block the path into the woods, as agreed. As he passed through the open gate and motored to his post, Tork wondered if he needed to spur his own horse into some kind of trot: he needed to block the main track back to school beyond Paul and turn the cows into the Grecian Valley. Those steers moved pretty quickly in the movies, and he didn't want to be overtaken before he got to his position. He twisted in his saddle to look over his shoulder, but the crest of the hill had nothing on it yet. This was a rural England summer's day, and those cows were taking their time ambling through their pasture, and the boys were not firing their six-guns into the air nor embarking on a thousand-mile drive.

"I'll shut the gate after." Paul reassured Tork that he knew his task as the horse shambled past.

"You're the king of the ranch-hands." Tork gave him the thumbs-up, then touched his non-existent hat instead in a single-finger salute, and let the horse pick his own way further along the track. Soon he pulled on the reins and turned the horse side-on to the track, looked down the Grecian valley in all its splendour, soon to receive a city of grazing beast, then back at Paul in post, then up to the crest in the field, waiting for the cows to appear.

Insects buzzed and hovered over the grass and in the still air under the trees. A beetle warily crossed the dusty stones of the track, and birds called across the landscaped valley that led to its magnificent folly, a huge temple standing majestically at the school end. Everything waited.

The yip-yip call became audible in the same moment as the first of the cattle appeared on the horizon: heads first, then bodies, then more heads behind and the first of the legs. Tork wished he'd thought to bring a cine camera, or better still a videotape one, just for that image. But he memorised it instead as more cattle appeared and then horse-riders to either side of them, and one behind. Tork almost gasped with admiration as one of the side-riders effortlessly moved into a canter that eased him past the cattle and through the gateway before them, then out wide again to stop, turn and watch the herd through. The rider at the back had shifted his position to compensate, and the one on the other side slowed to brake the movement as the cattle narrowed through the gap. It was like watching a flow of water or a single snake-like organism passing an obstacle: it was beautiful.

At twenty-five head it was a small herd by wild western standards, but as they spilled into the valley and whirled away in eddies to come to rest and sniff at the new grass, the feel of it was the same as that safe arrival after a mighty cross-continent trek. Paul's engine sprang into life and he trundled up to shut the gate. The three boys walked their horses down to join Tork.

"Great job, lads – thanks. You looked like proper cowboys."

They grinned. Ben spoke. "Enjoyed it. Did you say you wanted some sheep moved as well?"

Tork twisted and waved an arm behind him. "Those guys in there. We'll have to get them through up by the trees round the assault course, then we can walk them round the end of the ha-ha and down this track to the grass either side of the main drive."

John nodded. "If I'd known we were moving sheep I'd have brought my dog."

Tork leaned forward. "You have your own sheepdog?"

John looked surprised by the question. "I've got three. Well, one's my brother's technically, but he doesn't know what to do with it, and isn't interested neither, so she's pretty well mine as well. But I wasn't talking about them – they're home in Northumberland."

Tork nodded. "Right – so?"

John explained. "Well my lurcher's at school, isn't he?"

"Is he?"

"Yes, of course. It's a privilege for the Master of the Hounds. I keep him with the kennel huntsman."

Tork finally understood. "Oh, the beagles, of course – and you're the Master - I see. I didn't know about the special privilege that came with the post, though."

John passed over Tork's incomprehensible ignorance. "Probably for the best I didn't get him anyway. He's better at taking rabbits than rounding up sheep, really."

Ben pointed to the spot by the assault course. "Isn't the gate over there – the one you wanted us to bring the sheep through – isn't it usually locked?"

Paul was just arriving and Tork waited until the engine noise died. "Paul, Ben was asking if that gate over there was locked."

Paul grinned and fished around in a bag tied to the seat. He brought out a pair of bolt-cutters. "Not now!" He waved them happily then brought out the chain.

Tork turned to Ben. "Okay?"

"Okay, sir! Come on, boys."

The three of them rode off to the farmland, and Tork and Paul watched them go for a while. Eventually, Tork turned.

"I reckon we can leave them to it." Paul nodded and faced him. Tork nodded down the valley. "You and I need to go and build some milking stalls. That's the easy bit. Then this afternoon we're going to have to teach some boys to milk cows!"

Paul grinned.

Breadmaking

There were only three girls playing tennis, so it had been tempting to simply join in, but Alison had promised Deborah that she'd check on the breadmaking, so once the girls seemed okay playing a rotation of American doubles she left. The afternoon sun was dry and hot, and the game would soon become lethargic, but they'd have been out in the air and had a bit of a game at least. It was silly having only three of them playing when both the shop courts were available to them, but much to Alison's horror, all the other girls had genuinely wanted to have a go at baking bread.

She walked quickly through the cool under the few trees then stepped into the full sun radiating off stone and tarmac on her way to the south front of the mansion. The brightness and heat chased her all the way to the little servants' entrance that accessed Sub Street, the windowless avenue that ran the length of the building under the grand state rooms. She slowed a little while her eyes adjusted to the light, then tackled the stairs, swinging up and around to emerge into the splendour of the first floor with its incredibly high ceilings and the huge, interconnecting rooms of an eighteenth century summer palace built to impress. The first dining room felt like a cooler version of the tennis court despite shafts of sunlight streaming in the fabulously tall casement windows of the south front, and she strode along the sprung oak floors towards the servery. Gradually the rhythm of the thud of her footsteps was confused by the occasional off-beat, and Alison surprised herself by recognising the sound of wet dough being thrown on to a hard surface before she picked up the trill and giggle of girls' voices also coming from the second dining hall.

The servery was a much smaller room with an anomalous collection of steel surfaces and eye-level lights, but passing through into the far dining hall caught Alison's breath like a moment in a film when our hero stumbles into an earlier time. She'd never seen before the dark blinds pulled halfway down so that the sunshine had to bounce its way in and light the scene from underneath, giving it a Dutch-interior-style other-worldliness. The girls were all shockingly uniform, three standing at each of the huge dining tables, their distinctive variations of hair all tucked away inside white catering caps, their sleeves all rolled, their bodies wrapped in identical white aprons. They slapped and kneaded dough through a thin veil of flour dust billowing from the table tops and hanging transfixed in the sunlit air. They were busy, concentrating on working the soggy dough, but chatting and comparing as well. Greg, in a white lab coat, was wandering through their ranks, encouraging and advising. He should have been wearing a white smock: the tenant farmer ensuring the milkmaids got their baking work done before the cows called them away again, making the most of his lordship's labour force. Alison, as often before in her first year in this remarkable public school, was befuddled in a disorientating mist of disbelief, allure, mistrust and romance created by the image that greeted her.

Then the personalities popped through the whitened painting. "Hi, Miss." A kitchen girl who looked just like Kate seemed to be enjoying herself. Better still, Emily was grinning fit to burst.

"Hi, Kate, Emily. Is that better than drawing mechanical parts all afternoon?"

Emily glowed through the dust and lit up with another smile. "Honestly, Miss, I'm loving it." She hammered the ball of dough with the heel of her hand and tried to half-roll, half-slide it forward. "It's hard work, though - you'd be surprised!" She tried to curl her fingers around the end of it to bring it back on itself, but seemed to succeed only in ripping it. "And difficult!" she added, in inexplicable pleasure.

Greg appeared. "Like this," he said, without any further greeting or comment, rolling and folding back the dough ball with what appeared to be a single movement. Emily gave a snort of pleased laughter at the simple dexterity of his demonstration. "It's just practice. You don't need to scrabble your fingers around the end, look, it comes back on itself anyway - because of its own consistency – its stickiness, if you like." He did it twice more, then left it for Emily. "Hello, Miss Lawrenson – are you going to have a go yourself? There's plenty of flour, yeast and water…" Alison grinned but shook her head, she didn't know exactly why.

"No, thanks."

"Okay. Perhaps if you wash your hands anyway, that way you can leap in and help wherever you get the chance." Greg was waving towards the kitchens, and she was just turning to go when he kept talking. "The girls are doing really well. They're naturals. We had some boys in this morning, but…" he shook his head ruefully.

Alison nodded. "They're talented girls: they can do anything. And enjoy it too. Perhaps you could run some sort of inter-house baking competition?" Greg looked astounded. "I'll just…" She headed off to find somewhere to wash her hands, wondering what it was about his manner that had ruffled her.

Coming back, a shriek from Fiona and Sass caused her to head straight for them. Fiona saw her coming and rather obviously threw herself down on the mixture in front of her, whereupon both she and Sass erupted into gales of laughter. Alison threw a quick look over her shoulder, wondering if Greg were watching, and quickened her pace a little. "What's got into you two?" she asked with a broad smile.

They looked sideways at each other and howled anew.

Alison waited a few seconds. "Alright, alright – don't disturb the whole room. What are you two up to?"

Sass spluttered. "Not me, Miss – ask her!" She pointed frantically at Fiona and her mixture. "Ask her what she did with her – her doughy stuff…"

Fiona widened her eyes. "Me? I didn't do anything. I was just rubbing it like everyone else is…" Sass laughed. Fiona smiled. "And it just sort of stood up." They both burst out afresh. Alison sighed, gave them a minute.

"Okay, you two, get over it."

"Sorry, Miss." They made a show of bringing themselves under control. "It's okay..." they stood up straight. Fiona looked under her hand. "It's flaccid now..."

Hysteria. Alison looked around. Phoebe looked disapproving, Alexis was smiling and giggling a little. Ruth was shaking her head smilingly, Beth was craning her neck, looking as if she wanted to come and join in the fun. Greg had his back to them, but must have been able to hear.

Alison moved around and stood between them. "Come on, come on, that's enough now. Let's have a look at how you're doing – you need some flour down on the table, don't you? Let's see... oh, dear..."

Fiona shrugged. Her dough had become a wet, sticky mess. Sass had managed to get hers to disintegrate into tiny bits. "We actually don't seem to be much good at this, Miss."

"You think?" The three of them looked sorrowfully at the two piles on the table. "Well, it seems to me that yours is too wet and yours is too dry, so... why don't we put them both together, bash it around a bit, then split it back into two?" She looked from side to side to see what the two girls thought.

Sass spoke first. "Sounds like Maths, Miss: add this to this, do that to it, change this part of it, take away the number you first thought of."

Alison nodded. "Actually – you're not so far wrong. We're going to discard the individual values and use an arithmetical mean." Fiona gave the 'straight over my head' sign. "Oh, come on, don't play dumb. You know what an average is."

"Average?" Fiona set herself up. "Never heard the word."

"Yes!" Sass reacted. "Fifteen love, Miss."

Alison smiled and took the dough off them. "If you say so." She balled the two lumps together and started pummelling it. "They say it helps if you imagine it's someone who's got it coming." She threw it down on the table and started kneading it.

"Wow – so who are you thinking about, Miss?"

"Not Mr Rawlins, hopefully." Sass and Fiona met eyes behind Alison's back.

"What?" Alison didn't stop.

"Mr Rawlins, Miss. Isn't he your boyfriend, Miss?"

Now she stopped. She looked from side to side. "Why would you say that?"

Fiona shrugged. "It's the word on the street."

"Well, it's nonsense."

Sass chipped in. "You did take him a cup of coffee to the gate, Miss."

Alison felt suddenly breathless. "I think you'll find that's a long way short of a proof."

Sass turned her head slightly aside, almost a wink. "I think you'll find it's pretty conclusive, Miss. Don't you think, Fi?"

Fiona nodded wisely. "Sounds pretty conclusive to me. Then..." she held up her finger, "Mr Rawlins didn't deny it."

"Didn't deny what?"

Again the half turn of the head. "That you and he – you know..."

Alison felt herself slipping into a quagmire. "Well, he should have. I mean I'm sure he did. Oh, the whole thing is nonsense. Here..." she split the dough in two and slapped a ball down in front of each. "Give this a good pummelling and turn your overactive imaginations off."

But as she moved away she heard the words behind her, "Methinks the lady doth protest too much". She turned and glared at the two of them. They both affected innocence. Alison tried to put them out of mind, and to suppress the sense of irritation and helplessness.

"How are you two getting on?" She approached Becks and Kay, both of whom were evolving a product that looked very much like the dough of a practised baker.

"Hi, Miss," Becks opened her hands and gestured at the fruit of her labours sitting on the table-top. "What do you think? Pretty good, eh?"

Alison nodded appreciatively. "Looks fantastic, Becks – yours too, Kay. You guys really seem to have the knack of this. What happens next?"

Kay explained. "We leave it under a damp tea towel for a couple of hours and it grows like magic."

"Then pop it in the oven and hope!" Becks added.

Alison smiled at their enthusiasm. "And you're obviously finding the whole experience enjoyable?"

"Oh, Miss..." Becks gave an odd smile. "It just makes you want to go straight out, have unprotected sex and grow babies!"

She opened her eyes wide at Alison, who suddenly noticed that Becks was rounder and heavier than most of the girls. She looked bovine. Alison shook her head to dispel the image. "Oh, Becks, really... is that honestly the limit of your ambition?"

"No, Miss," she and Kay glanced smilingly at each other, "good-looking husband, really nice house..."

"...*really* nice..."

"...and lots of friends..."

"...lots!"

Alison gazed at the two of them. She never knew, on this topic, if they just liked winding her up, or if they actually meant it.

End of Day One

Tork stowed his climbing gear away more securely in the bottom of the box. Normally he liked to have it handy for work on the roof, but the weather had been so dry and fine for so long now that it was easy moving around the stone pedestals and balustrades, the struts, supports and bits of kit that littered the area, even at night. The co-operative moon lit the obstacles under his feet and bathed the heat-parched grounds for miles in every direction.

Perching on the brick ledge of a low chimney stack, Tork surveyed the silver-gilt estate, its mirror-flat lawns at the mansion's foot, its shining lake darkening further the rise behind it to the silhouette of the magnificent arch black against the night sky. He turned to face the Grecian valley, trying to sense the presence of the cattle there, but heard only the sheep on the main course and the creakings and workings of the house closing down for the night. The occasional voice. He breathed. It had been a good day: one to treasure.

He tested the stability of a short flagpole, then used it to swing himself down. Time to go.

Most of the housemasters had already joined the Head in Elizabeth's office by the time the television clicked into life.

"Ah-ha," said several, as they adjusted their position slightly to better see the screen.

The BBC news signature tune and graphics duly rolled by, then the same unfamiliar newsreader as the night before appeared. There was no news besides the pandemic, and apart from some footage of full hospital wards, it was less news than it was government instructions. Emergency powers had been passed and parliament suspended: government was working from Chequers. There was no address by the Prime Minister. The state of emergency was expected to last two weeks in the first instance, subject to the progress of the disease. Everyone was to stay home except for members of certain government agencies, or those directly requested by those same agencies. Food dumps would be set up and local areas alerted to their location and arrangements. The national grid and water supply were expected to continue uninterrupted; some telephone connections had gone down but were under repair. Hospitals should not be contacted, but anyone with a distinctive, blotchy red rash forming a complete ring around the neck or a limb should ring 999 immediately. Stay home; speak or open the door to no-one without government ID; visit a food dump only if you must.

Click.

The Head, who had one of the three armchairs in the room, got to his feet and turned to the assembled company. "It sounds rather more serious than I had hoped." He looked to Elizabeth and then around the room. "Are we all assembled? Is Tork here?" Tork waved from the back, one of the latecomers who had slipped in during the broadcast. "Let's go next door, then." He made his way through them and entered his office. The housemasters paused to allow Elizabeth and Deborah to go in next.

"Blimey, it's *The Roses of Eyam*," said Tony, whose house had put the play on a year previously, as they filed through and settled themselves amid serious looks and hushed expectancy.

"Well," Whitley began. "Thank you for coming." He paused, lost for a second with no more routine to shelter in. "I – I don't think the news bulletin offers us much, but there are some useful nuggets: plan for two weeks' duration in the first place; watch for that rash; hope for, but don't expect, the phones again; keep turning everyone away at the gate; food dumps…" He stopped counting off items on his fingers and looked at the faces around him. "I'm not sure what the message is about food dumps. They'll let us know where they are but don't want us to go. And we can't exactly nip down and quickly grab a couple of things that'll keep us going for a week or so: there are more than 500 of us on site." Everyone seemed to expect a proposal from him. "Look, I think there's a lot we can do in our normal way: ensure the continuation of security arrangements; devise a programme for the next two weeks; decide how to watch for symptoms and how to respond if we find them; come up with a communication plan with parents... There are logistics that we must and can do. But first, I want to have ten minutes on food, and I want to hear how you think the boys – and girls," he gestured briefly to Deborah, "are. How are they? What are they thinking?"

The housemasters found it oddly disconcerting at first to be asked so directly about the thoughts and feelings of their boys by such an earnest-looking Headmaster. John blustered a little. "They're fine, Headmaster. They just get on with it. One or two of them will need watching, but most boys... they won't dwell on it as long as we keep things moving."

"It may seem a little insensitive," Roger threw John a sideways look before continuing, "but essentially I think John's absolutely right. They'll be okay as long as their own routine – the one the school provides for them – is maintained. It'll be a nuisance having no sports fixtures to prepare for, but the novelty of the helping-out activities will compensate a bit. Blitz spirit. And having a few staff absent will allow us to get revision on their agenda. Keep them occupied, they'll be fine – like always."

"Perhaps a few extra housematches?" Tony wondered. "Maybe eliminate just one house each round instead of half of them – keep more involved."

"Some boys are alright," Dominic returned to the actual question, "but some clearly aren't. They're not saying anything, but they're turning in on themselves, especially the ones who aren't engaged by sport and the like."

"The Art School has always been a good home to the sensitive few. There must be a way we can encourage that," Michael pondered. "And perhaps cultivate the Music Department to try and do the same?"

"The peripatetic staff are largely off-site, of course," Dominic observed.

"Maybe a second house drama festival?" Tony suggested.

Chris chortled. "My boys are fine – it would be me I'd be worrying about if we had another drama festival. I haven't got over the last one yet."

"Deborah?" Whitley asked.

She shrugged. "I'm not sure continuous activity works so well with sixth-form girls, although a lot of them did enjoy the bread-making, apparently. They're worrying. And they'll make each other worse, I think."

Whitley nodded in a manner intended to appear both wise and sympathetic before turning to the only one not to have spoken. "Simon?"

Simon sat forward. "Um – I don't think they've thought about half-term yet. I think as long as they're working on the assumption that this is just a temporary thing – almost a drill – that they put up with for a while then go home, then we're fine. But as half-term draws nearer they'll expect some contact with parents, I think."

Whitley nodded. "Yes. So, I think we're saying we may have a sort of grace period with the boys, but perhaps a little less so with the girls. What about food, Philip?"

The Bursar somehow came to attention while still sitting in his chair. "Geoff gave me a walk-round. Obviously some things – milk, bread – are daily deliveries, so we'll run out of those immediately, although we do have decent stocks of dried milk and flour, dried fruits and so forth. And we have a good stock of canned goods, and the freezers are full. We have significant reserves against the possibility of temporary delivery failure, but only for a day or two – not two weeks, or anything like."

Brick sought clarification, "A day or two? And we've already had one, so we run out tomorrow?"

Philip wavered. "If it were just a day or two, then we, the consumers, wouldn't really notice much difference. But then that would be it. If, on the other hand, the catering quality and quantity changes radically straight away - we go to emergency rations in effect – then that could buy us a few days more. I haven't done a proper stock-take on other sources – CCF, D of E, house kitchens, perhaps even some private individuals – but I'd be surprised if they changed the picture much."

Again, Whitley nodded, then turned to Tork. "The farm?"

Tork sat forward. "We went and got ourselves a decent milking herd this morning, and some of the boys are getting the hang of the actual milking process. We wasted a lot at first, but I think we could produce a tolerable amount of milk on a regular basis now, once we've built a few more stalls and as long as we don't end up butchering and eating the cattle, of course. We've got sheep for meat in the first instance..."

Michael interrupted, "I don't understand – how did we just get hold of these animals?"

John was on a different tack. "Butchering them? Do we have the skills and facilities for that? Or the licence?"

Tork pressed on. "They're all from the parts of the estate let to tenant farming. Butchering them won't be to international standards, but we can manage perfectly well. Mankind did a fair bit of it before international standards. Then we also have good stocks of grain, and once we've built a milling machine we should be able to provide enough flour to keep the bread-making going."

"That bread this evening was good," added Chris.

"We may need to try growing yeast sooner or later, I don't know if the Biology department could do that?" Tork looked at John.

John looked at the Head. "Aren't we going a bit fast here, Headmaster? Dabbling with butchery and growing your own fungal products is not without its hazards. Especially with no hospitals or other medical help beyond sister in the san, we don't want to embark on anything unsafe."

Whitley gazed back at him. "We're just talking, John – but I'm not sure any of the options open to us are going to be safe, as such. People talk about not doing things unless they're 100% safe, but there is no such thing, after all. Today's unacceptable risk may be tomorrow's necessity."

"Does the tenant farmer know we've got his animals?" Michael asked.

"How risky is butchering your own meat?" Roger wanted to know.

"Some pigs would be good," Tony was thinking of bacon.

"Did the girls make that bread?" Chris asked Deborah.

"Have we got enough sheep to get to half term anyway?" Simon wondered, as Deborah beamed and nodded at Chris.

"Or chickens," Dominic was looking at Tony.

"Jolly good!" Chris stage-whispered towards Deborah with a thumbs-up sign.

Tork held his hands up. "There's one big question we need to answer before any of these others, and that's the one the Head was introducing when he said that the risk we decline today may become our best bet tomorrow. Do we plan for two weeks only, keeping normality as close as possible and gambling everything on rescue arriving before bust does, or do we go straight for radical change and something sustainable? Or else do we chart some middle course where we slide from normality into higher risk step by step?" He gave them all a moment. "Do we eat the grain, or plant it, or both?" He waited until one of them – it was Roger – was about to speak, presumably about grain, and then he cut him off. "Do we eat the cow, or keep the supply of milk?" He paused again. "Do we take risks today, or never, or only when we're desperate?"

There was a sober pause. Whitley felt it was his job to move on from it. "Thank you, Tork: I think that's absolutely right." Elizabeth gazed at Tork so hard that it drew his own eyes to her. She smiled briefly and looked back down at her notes. "Naturally we all hope that half term will bring a restoration of normality, but it's clear we can't depend on that – we may even have the boys and girls still with us over the holiday and beyond. We seem to have stocks enough of food and of the boys' natural thoughtless resilience for a week or so, but then we can expect a week of deep anxiety and possible hardship. And then there may be another week, and another: we don't know. Eventually we will have to consider not only our attitudes to the health and safety of food provision, but to lawlessness – that of those who may visit us, and that of ourselves." Several quizzical looks being thrown his way, Whitley explained. "Dominic wants chickens." He glanced and smiled at Dominic. "How long before we decide to risk a raid on the chicken factory not three miles from here?"

This was received as a food-for-thought rhetorical question, although it may well have been looking for an actual answer expressed in hours or days or weeks. The housemasters looked sombrely at each other. No-one looked at Tork, so no-one noticed that his eyes were shining.

Eventually Roger spoke. "This will end. And it is up to us that we are seen to have behaved well."

"Hear, hear," added Brick. Some nods. Some looking uncomfortable but unable to say anything that followed on, until Dominic cleared his throat.

"As it seems to have fallen to me to make the case for chicken..." he paused for an acknowledgement of his little joke, "I think we just need to be clear. We're saying that rather than being seen as selfishly concerned only with ourselves, and getting to the chickens first, we'd rather wait until someone else has already robbed the chicken factory, and go then – possibly too late – or perhaps not go at all?" He looked about him and seemed to see an accusation. "I'm not saying that we should go and steal chickens tonight, for goodness' sake, but I am just checking that we're saying that we'd rather – we'd rather die than lead the rush – that reputation is more important than survival... that we'd let some of the boys become ill or even die rather than be the school that began the looting?"

Some looked down, others wordlessly expressed impatience. None found the right form of words, but Roger felt he had been called out so replied. "Yes." This, too, appeared to get a mixed reception.

Elizabeth put her pen in the air like a schoolchild with a question. "Can I..? I'm just... are we discussing whether or not to rob the chicken factory, or is that some kind of metaphorical example of something?"

Whitley said evenly, "I don't think the discussion needs minuting in that kind of detail."

John stirred. "We're leaders. We train leaders: it's in our DNA. So we abide by rules and a moral code."

"Hear, hear," added Brick.

It was clear no-one was going to argue, though less clear how a vote would go, should it have been undertaken. Brick consolidated won ground, "So no robbing or looting – which has the additional benefit of everyone staying on site, minimising the possibility of infection." He glanced at Elizabeth to suggest that maybe that was worth minuting.

"So what's out strategy – until half-term, at least?" Simon asked.

"Headmaster," Philip began, "I think we should begin by closing all food outlets except the dining hall, and moving any stocks we have in the school shop or the CCF store or anywhere else into the main kitchens where the caterers can take charge of it. Geoff can then assess what there is and come up with a menu that provides the basic minimum of rations – same for everyone – for as long as possible, supplemented with whatever bread, milk, baking or dairy products we can improvise."

"Good by me," Tork interjected, "although the grain needs to stay at the farm where it can be stored properly. We'll keep the sheep in reserve, and come up with a plan to secure the geese, duck and any other wildfowl we have on the estate. And I'd like to sow some of the grain."

The warmth of response generated by the wildfowl comment turned to ashes of bafflement. It was Michael who vocalised it. "Sow some of it? But there's no point in that unless – unless this goes on for at least a year?"

"And we couldn't keep it up for a year anyway," Simon added.

"That's exactly why we do it," Tork concluded enigmatically. No-one understood him so he explained. "Not doing it says exactly that – we're all doomed within a year anyway. Doing it says that if we have to go self-sufficient, then we'll do so, no problem. It's going to be okay."

"But that's not true, is it?"

"Who knows?" Tork tackled Simon's question. "It may or may not be. Would you rather tell them we've decided to let them die to preserve the school's reputation?"

"Oh, for God's sake..."

"Alright, John," Whitley intervened, "I don't like Tork's paraphrase either," he gave Tork a warning look, "but he raises a fair point: what exactly are we going to tell the boys and girls, once they start asking?"

"More or less the truth, I suppose," Michael suggested, "that we don't really know much more than they do, that we're in lockdown for a couple of weeks, and that everything should be okay by half-term."

"They'll accept that," Chris observed.

"In assembly, maybe," Dominic conceded, "but not one-to-one or in smaller groups: they'll push to know what else we've heard, and ask how we know it'll all be okay by half-term..."

"Absolutely," Deborah added.

"And if they don't get answers from us, they'll push other members of staff," Simon pointed out.

"I wonder..." Tony paused. "Some of mine seem to have formed the idea that it's all some sort of drill that we're implementing. Maybe we should simply allow that to gather a bit of momentum? It would act as a reassurance."

"Gosh," said Michael, "so the conspiracy theorists would be the ones calming everyone else down. That would be a twist."

"Irony on the appearance and reality nexus – Shakespeare's obsessive theme." Roger glanced over to English-teacher Simon to check he'd spotted his erudition.

"They may break bounds if they think it's just an exercise." Brick warned, more practically.

"Or worse," Dominic added. "Some of them know about the Robbers Cave experiment, and that it was condemned as unethical to practise experiments on unwitting subjects. We do it in my Introduction to Psychology General Studies course. They could challenge us quite openly."

"If they break bounds, they could bring the disease back with them." Brick returned to what he saw as the more essential considerations. "So we can't let them think this is just some exercise."

"Then perhaps, if pushed," Simon looked around him, "we should just talk to them – tell them the whole truth about this discussion, the different things we have to weigh up, the difficulty of making decisions on inadequate information, of anticipating the reactions of others, the way you need to be ready to review and change policy as you go along..."

Deborah gave a little snort of derision. "The girls wouldn't cope with that – and they're not so different from the boys as most of you tend to suppose, their responses are just a little more visible, that's all. They're all children still, and they need some credible reassurance to get through this."

John, his chivalric gallantry pricked, leapt in. "Quite right. We tell them it's two weeks then back to normal. And if we have to tell them something different in two weeks, then we do that, but meanwhile we show a bit of conviction: we know what we're doing, we've got it covered, we're all agreed, this is how we get through this. Now that's leadership – strong, decisive, confident. Something you can have faith in. What you call the other thing – wringing your hands, saying you don't really know, explaining difficulties, admitting differences of opinion – I really wouldn't know."

Tork timed it perfectly. "An education?" he suggested.

Part Three

Poaching

So the Bramblingums were told that the self-sufficiency and isolation operation would go on for two weeks, and that half-term arrangements would be announced in due course. And they went with that. They discussed it amongst themselves when it occurred to them to do so, argued themselves uncertain about how real it all was, and forgot about it the rest of the time. The occasional sudden realisation that this event would be cancelled or that one would be affected led to the situation being bewailed or celebrated, as appropriate, but not usually to its being subjected to further examination. They worried vaguely and intermittently about their parents and families, but there was nothing really to be said about that, so they didn't discuss it much.

Meanwhile the changes to routine were a continual subject of speculation, debate and opinion. Most innovations reduced the dominance of ordinary lessons and prep in their lives, which was not unwelcome. Many of the more academic pupils were pleased of the chance to get back into the Design workshops, or in other ways to apply their skills to immediate practical problems. They enjoyed the opportunity to explore more widely a range of topics of their own choice as the curriculum became inevitably more project-based: practical projects needed doing around the school, and setting research projects was a good way of coping with cover lessons and absent or double-booked teachers. Some of the Upper Sixth – the final-year pupils - expressed some concern about their exam preparation and university entrance, but it was the same for everyone, presumably. The less academic enjoyed the change of emphasis not only for its own sake, but because they sensed themselves becoming more central to the school's operation. Most enjoyed the new challenges laid before them, as long as they could approach them with a reasonable expectation of success.

Gerry and Tadhg liked to set themselves their own challenges. They had their own vision of their last term at Brambling College, and it included very little A level revision and a lot of appreciation of the possibilities of the grounds in summer and the relative freedom of Upper Sixth formers to explore them. They also had their own ferret, purse nets, primus stove, oil, pan and bottles of claret, all hidden away in their study. They reckoned that little nuggets of rabbit meat fried in breadcrumbs might work well, given the facilities available. And they'd spotted a likely burrow in the woods near the athletics track, out of sight of any of the boarding houses.

Annoyingly, however, it had become much more difficult to predict who would be where when, and hence harder to embark on nefarious activities that needed to be free of interruption. "What are you guys up to, then?" was not a question you wanted to hear just when you had all your purse nets staked in place and Freddie the illegal stowaway ferret raring to go.

Thus it was that at two o'clock in the morning of a moonless night their torchlight could just about be seen in the depths of the woods off the path by the athletics track. Freddie waited in his carrying cage as Gerry and Tadhg moved as silently as they could between the different rabbit holes they had previously mapped in their minds. Snap too many twigs, make too easily detectable vibrations in the earth, be too obvious, and all the rabbits would bolt out of the one hole you'd missed, Freddie disappearing into the dark after them. They'd figured all this out, never having hunted with a ferret at night before themselves. But Tadhg was sure it was done in Ireland, and the rest, surely, was just a matter of using your wits and experience.

They crept back together and whispered. "What d'you reckon?"

Their beams tracked back and forth over the nearby ground. "There's probably another somewhere, but no way of finding it now. At least one of them should come out of a netted hole, even if we lose a couple out of one we missed."

"As long as we don't lose Freddie. It could take all night to try and get him back."

There was no more to be said, really. But then, suddenly, Tadgh was alert. "Turn your torch off."

Gerry did so; Tadgh already had. They stood in silent darkness. Gerry sensed Tadgh straining to listen, so he waited for a while before asking, "What?"

Tadgh waited before answering. "Thought I heard something."

"A patrol?"

"Dunno."

Gerry left it a minute. "Amateurs. They only operate up to about midnight – this is past their bedtime. Anyway, they're just patrolling the borders." They waited a little longer in silence. "Okay – no-one there. Let's get Freddie on the job."

The night air had a slight chill on it after so warm a day, and they were glad of the hunting jackets they had worn mainly for their capacious pockets. Even when there had been enough time for their night-sight to kick in, and even though there were stars above the trees somewhere, it was too dark to see anything without a torch. Gerry turned his on, but with his hand over the beam to control the spill of light. Freddie seemed to have lost interest, and may even have been thinking of going back to sleep. When Gerry opened the cage the ferret walked up his arm and stood on his shoulders. "Watch it," said Tadgh, "he might fall and break his neck."

"Doesn't seem to be expecting a hunt at this time," Gerry observed. "He'll be alright once we put his nose in a hole. Have you got that spade?" Freddie being male, there was always the possibility he might have to be dug out and persuaded not to eat the rabbit himself below ground.

"Here." Tadgh put on his torch and picked up the short spade. Gerry placed his own torch beam-down on the ground and used both hands to get Freddie off his shoulders.

"Shine yours on the hole, can you?" The lead hole was spotlit and Gerry held Freddie close to it. The little animal wriggled and got his legs going. "He's excited. Rabbits definitely still in there. Ready?"

Tadgh, unseen, nodded. Gerry released Freddie down the hole and picked up his torch. You could hear little feet and movement under the earth, like a tiny tremor. The two warped circles of light at the end of the torchbeams shot around the ground, resting briefly on each purse net before dashing on. The screeching started as rabbits reacted, filling the air under the tree branches eerily. Suddenly a net burst into a wriggling bag as a dark, furry, explosion of panic filled and stretched it. "Got one!" said Tadgh, dropping the torch and pulling the drawstring free of the peg. His boots were illuminated as he swung the spade in one hand at the bag in the other. The rabbit became deadweight. Tadgh dropped it, grabbed the torch in time to see Freddie appear where the net had been. He came out and probably would have turned to go back, but seemed surprisingly compliant when Tadgh picked him up and put him back in his cage. Gerry was round the other side of the burrow.

"Damn – there they go." A couple of bobbing scuts flashed in the torchlight through the undergrowth. "Oh, but hang on..." a young rabbit lay frozen in another purse net. Gerry got the bag off the pegs and, checking the draw string was secure, lobbed the bag at Tadgh who, unsurprisingly, missed it. It landed beside him on the ground, where he gave it a sharp tap with the spade. The other nets were empty, although one had been sprung.

"Two and the ferret back – settle for that."

"Yup." Gerry started packing up the nets. "Don't you break their necks?"

"Sometimes. Not if I've got a spade in my hand."

"Are you sure they're dead?"

Tadgh got the rabbits out of the nets for a look. "Yup." He put them on the ground and folded away the nets. They packed up the rest of the gear, loaded their pockets and looked around. Tadgh had the rabbits by the feet in his hand.

"Let's have a look." Tadgh held them up. "One's a bit small, but a good night's work. Can't wait to fry them up with a bit of vino."

Torches scanning the ground ahead, they stepped carelessly through the twiggy ground, no longer worried about a bit of noise and light – not until they were nearer school, anyway. They were kings of the wood, top of the food chain.

Two torches came on, directed straight into their faces, just as they regained the path. "Caught you!"

"Who's that?" Gerry peered over his shielding hand to see what his own torch could pick out, and recognised Tom. "Winters? What d'you think you're doing here?" He moved his torch beam to try and identify the second person. "And Stuart Viceman for god's sake?"

"Wiseman," Stuart corrected.

"What's the Lower Sixth doing sneaking around the woods at night?"

"Catching the Upper Sixth poaching, apparently."

Gerry prepared to move on. "Well, there's only enough for us, so you're out of luck."

"You're the one out of luck – you're bust."

Gerry pretended he was looking around him. "Bust? Oh, dear me. Bust by who?"

"Us – patrol."

Gerry looked sideways at Tadgh then menacingly at Tom. "Yes, but you're not on your little soldier playing patrol games, are you? You're not in uniform and you haven't got one of your back-up teacher officers with you, have you? In fact..." he moved closer into

Tom's face, "you're not even supposed to be here, are you? I think it's us that's bust you, lower sixth boy."

Tom was steady. "We heard you leave house and went to check on you. Smudge will be impressed by our initiative. It's a good bust – could make one of us Head of House next year instead of Blanco, and that's got to be worth it."

"Worth it? Worth it? Don't cross us, soldier boy. Tadgh's Irish, you know."

"He lives in Chelsea."

Tadgh spoke up. "That's just a flat for when we need to do business in London."

"You always need to do business in London, then," Stuart pointed out.

"Look," Gerry was becoming exasperated, "we're not sharing, and you're not grassing. End of discussion. If anyone hears anything about this, you will definitely regret it. The Upper Sixth will make your life hell. Get back to bed. Except wait a few minutes so we get back first. Come on, Tag."

They walked off, two insignificant lights wavering on the path for a while, then snuffing out round a corner.

"Well, that went well. Maybe leave me out next time," said Stuart ruefully.

"You don't want to tell Smudge, then?"

Stuart tried to explain. "I don't know how he'll react – Gerry may be right that he'll be more pissed with us for being out than pleased about the bust. And he may not even be pleased about the bust anyway – they tend to want to leave the Upper Sixth to it in the last term. But we *do* know how the Upper Sixth will react." He paused. "So no, I don't think I want to tell him. Maybe just let's go back to bed before they think of a way of ensuring we get caught trying to get back in."

"Shit," said Tom.

Two days later Chris happened to mention at the housemasters' meeting that he'd heard a whisper that some of his may have been up to a spot of poaching at night.

"Really?" asked Brick.

Chris shrugged. "Word on the street, as they say. And some rabbit remains and a claret bottle in the houseroom litter bin."

"Would you have a claret with rabbit?" Roger asked.

"Depends on the sauce," ventured Dominic.

Roger turned. "You think they made a sauce?"

Brick leant forward to engage Chris. "Are you going to be able to find out who it was?"

Chris looked knowing. "I think I know whose ear to have a quiet word in."

Whitley looked troubled. "I think we need to take it more seriously than that in present circumstances, Chris." He furrowed his brow with a thought that was only yet half-formed. "I mean, we're sharing resources that are very limited. This could be a very unpleasant development."

Chris looked alarmed. "They weren't looting, Headmaster – just night larks, really. I'm beginning to wish I hadn't mentioned it."

Tork got involved. "We don't need to punish them, do we? Can't we put them to work? If they're that good at catching rabbits then let's convert them from thieves in the night to honoured members of the community."

Chris looked pained. "They won't want that. It's a hobby with the additional frisson of illegality – a bit of fun, not work."

"Isn't turning their interests and hobbies into their work what we're trying to teach them to do?"

Everyone took a breath and a sidelong glance. Another show-stopper from Tork.

Eventually Simon spoke. "I wonder, when this is all over and we've come through it, if we should maybe set up some sort of committee to look into these questions that have arisen. Reconsider what we do and why."

This fell into the pool like a witch on trial who might sink or swim. Whitley found the idea quite attractive, but Brick started speculating how to set it up, and Brick was so completely the wrong man for this kind of committee that he made it lose its shine simply by talking about it. Chris was just relieved that the pressure was off his poachers, and so he encouraged more talk about how this committee could work. Roger showed his written notes to John:

Or we could leave the youngsters to talk bollocks on their own in the pub, as has always been done.

Philip

Philip had woken early with a feeling of being overwhelmed by work – a feeling he normally dispelled by spending an hour or two at his desk before the day proper began. However, on this occasion, despite the promising walk from his home in the beginnings of another spectacularly bright summer's day, he'd found nothing in his office that he could satisfactorily tick off a mental list. All the usual generators of paperwork had failed him, and he'd found nothing in his in-tray to which he could formulate an incisive and business-like reply to pass on to the secretarial staff by way of his out-tray. A feeble pile of memoranda, unswollen by any mail from the outside world, sat stubbornly in his in-tray, thinned only slightly by his transfers to the waste-paper bin, hardly at all by any movement to the out-tray, all insistently pending further discussion or information before action was possible, and none of them remotely important or even urgent. All the various strategy plans and policy reviews were effectively on hold; no official forms or returns would arrive and demand attention. The maintenance department and the Clerk of the Works had effectively joined forces with the Design Department, and were getting on with what had to be done without pressing him first for budget decisions. There were no staffing issues, and the phone wasn't going to ring.

He picked the phone up just in case a dialling tone would indicate that a connection had been restored, but no. The feeling of a huge swell of work building and threatening to overcome him remained, yet there was nothing he could do to pick any of it off in the countdown to d-day.

He made himself a cup of coffee and walked out of the French window through one of the many classical arches that made up the ground level of the South Front. The lawn between him and the balustrade was noticeably shaggier than usual: the ground staff, like the rest of the maintenance team, had all been deployed elsewhere in the grounds, supervising boys building enclosures for wildfowl, digging irrigation ditches, improving milking facilities, expanding the farm. He gazed down the southern vista, noting the subtly changed look of the cricket pitch, analysing the untidiness that had crept under the trees on either side. He normally took pride in the immaculate, clipped, polished look of this centre-piece of the grounds – good sign of a bursar doing his job well. But that was not available to him this morning.

Not that it was ever that straightforward: Bramblingums old and present and even honorary were strangely romantic about the place, and frequently objected to his clear-up operations. A permanent obstacle to all his earnest fund-raising for repairing follies, restoring temples, sorting out plantations and waterways was a sort of hazy, starry-eyed love of the mystery and lapsed grandeur of the grounds. They loved the young ash tree growing out from under the lead roof of the rotundo, the shady, shifting uncertainties under the self-seeded growth in the ruins of a couple of the classical temples, even the netting there to catch any falling masonry from the ornamentation of the arches. The overgrown held their longing and their breath in a way the trimmed and cared-for could never match.

Trouble was, it all added up to a growing financial crisis. They were a school, after all, and you couldn't allow buildings to become unsafe and start falling on pupils, even if it was partly their fault for climbing on them. And although Old Bramblingum fathers probably still longed for their boys to have access to the unspoiled playing fields of their own pasts, parents more generally expected schools to have more modern aspects and to prepare their charges for a newer world. If all available money kept going to educational progress, then the follies and beauties of the outer grounds were increasingly likely to end up bulldozed.

And then the pool of nostalgically loyal fathers with compliant wives and huge trust funds was too small to be the only one they were fishing in for prospective pupils: the roll was falling. They needed a way to fill the school to bursting with full fee-paying pupils, and to establish a separate income stream to run the estate. Maybe that was the undone work that was troubling him, but that had been an undercurrent for some time, and couldn't really explain his restlessness this particular morning.

Nothing for it but to wait until the day begins. Then, if the office did not immediately involve him in activity, he would walk the ship, as the naval types would say. Breathing the air as deeply as he could, his own unquiet remained below the calm thus induced. In best RAF tradition, he set about a systems-check as the sun warmed him.

Two smallish heads appeared above the greensward and drew his attention as swaying necks and PE shirts appeared below them, announcing a couple of third formers returning up the slope from a morning run. He watched them approach, heading for the ground floor entrance just by "his" lawn, hiding at the foot of the grand portico.

"Morning, boys," he called as they made their way to the door.

James and Charlie looked across at him. "Morning, sir."

"Punishment run?"

"No, sir – just fitness," James replied, opening the door.

"But," Charlie added, "if you'll vouch for us, maybe we could put it down as a credit in case we need it later?"

Philip smiled. As the boys went in, he noticed one of them was carrying a book. Perhaps a book of early morning exercise suggestions, but he doubted it.

"Who was that?" James asked.

"In charge of the money," Charlie explained as they headed back to house.

Philip returned to his self-evaluation. No, it wasn't work, as such. Running an isolated commune actually involved less admin. The work was simpler, somehow, and people just got on with it. There would be an aftermath later to deal with, but it wasn't work that was overwhelming him in the meanwhile.

He sipped his coffee and found himself looking past the Chapel – the route home. Deborah. A warning light came on. It was Deborah he was worrying about. He had expected to support her – he thought she'd worry herself sick about their two boys. "Good grief," she'd said. "We've done our job there – they're both sensible and each as strong as a horse. Service wives and mothers soon learn not to brood on anticipations of disaster." He still wasn't sure if he was impressed or appalled by this reaction. Perhaps just intimidated, even belittled.

She'd become a bit of a school ma'am, he supposed, since she took on the girls' house. Maybe it was that. He was proud of her for being selected and doing it so well, especially as she wasn't a teacher. He flushed slightly at the memory. They should have given it to Esther Nicholson, really. It had been Roger who'd pointed out that their first-ever housemistress would be called "Knickers" by the boys, and Philip remembered with discomfort the success of his own joke – that the sight of Esther's car disappearing down the drive would be greeted by the boys saying to the girls, "That's Knickers off, then!" He knew that he was trying to weaken Esther's application and thus strengthen Deborah's. It was unprofessional – even though it couldn't really have made any difference to the outcome. It had just popped into his head: he still wished he hadn't said it.

But it was such a good job for her and he hadn't wanted her idle now the boys were grown up – he'd been slightly afraid of her being bored. And now he felt that way again. Her friendship with Elizabeth had always unsettled him a little, and now that she was staying with them, it was more noticeable. They were odd together. There was an aura in the house of confidential innuendo and appraisal, in which he wasn't included. When Deborah was on duty and he was alone with Elizabeth, she seemed amused by him, as if he were the subject of a private joke she knew. His normal charm failed him.

There had been a time when Philip had been a dashing young RAF officer and, frankly, a bit of a flirt who didn't always stop there. But he'd been completely cured of all that by a horrifying brush with some "swingers" on a particular base where they had been stationed when the boys were at prep school. They'd attended what they'd supposed to be one of the normal drinks parties of military bases all over the commonwealth, and gradually realised the wife-swapping nature of the planned finale. He'd found Deborah, taken her aside, and asked her if she'd realised what was going on. "Of course," she'd said, and looked at him so directly he could still see the minutely precise and constant focus of her young eyes on his, "do you want us to stay?". Something inside him turned to jelly; he could still feel the sensation in his bowel when he brought that picture to mind.

Of course, he had never had a way of discovering definitively whether or not she had been bluffing. But an iron spike of insecurity had entered his soul anyway, and never shifted. She was stronger than him. His job became to ensure that the circumstances in which that mattered never arose: to provide a comfortable, unthreatening but interesting lifestyle whose order was not worth challenging. And Brambling had provided that – until now.

Whitley on the prowl

The Head had decided it was time he gave the farm a visit, seeing as it was now playing such a prominent part in life at Brambling. He should really go and look at the CDT department as well: his Director of Studies had just explained to him the various curriculum changes that had been made, and that the "practical activities" that had traditionally been a peripheral part of the academic programme at Brambling were now the centre of its gravity. He also wanted a bit of a frank chat with Tork away from the housemasters, and thought he'd get more out of him if he caught him on his own turf, so as to speak.

He looked around his desk and could see nothing on it to delay him: the notes Anthony had left him with the details of the discussed changes were handwritten, probably inscrutable, and presumably summarised by the explanation he'd just heard, so had little appeal. Other papers waiting to be read seemed painfully irrelevant until the present crisis was over. There was little point in trying to prepare some sort of report to parents without some idea of how to send it, and most daily business now got sorted with the housemasters at night, in the light – or gloom - of the latest broadcast, at least on those nights when there was one.

He drifted into Elizabeth's room, where the closing of the door indicated that Anthony had just left. Elizabeth pulled a face. Whitley interpreted it. "Anthony not happy?"

Elizabeth shrugged. "Needs must. But he doesn't like not feeling in control."

"Who does?" Whitley asked, rhetorically, he thought.

"People on roller coasters."

Whitley lifted both eyebrows. "Hadn't thought of that."

"They sell a lot of tickets."

"Yes," he replied meditatively. He wasn't sure if he was being told something, or just chatting inconsequentially. No matter. "Do you know if Tork is more likely to be at CDT or the farm?"

"Isn't it on Anthony's timetable?"

Whitley sighed. "Probably."

"Although Tork's whereabouts have never been entirely in accord with the timetable, I gather."

"You're right." Whitley was pleased of the excuse not to bother deciphering Anthony's scrawl. "I think I'll have a look at CDT anyway, then go on to the farm. Do I need to be back for anything in particular?"

Elizabeth waved a diary in the air. "Every item before lunch has a neat pencil-line straight through it – the morning is all yours."

"Remarkable."

"Do you want to take Nietzsche with you?" Whitley looked at the dog with alarm. "Only joking." She gave him a little wave and then peered at her computer screen. Whitley withdrew.

He felt curiously elated as he stepped out into the South Front sun, freed not only from his office, but from anyone he needed to impress or persuade or restrain. Just him strolling round his school on a little informal tour of inspection of some recent innovations. And checking with Tork that they weren't all going to starve before the week was out. The thought wasn't as overbearing as it should have been, and he wondered if he too had some of the thoughtless, privileged resilience that had been attributed to the boys.

He passed through the balustrade and beyond the foot of the steps, peering across the Bursar's lawn into the open French window of his office, hoping Philip wouldn't see him and hurry out with some annoying little piece of business. No sign of him. He continued into Chapel Court and was immediately struck by the hubbub of a group of Bramblingums coming his way from the classrooms.

It somehow didn't look like a normal change-over between lessons: this group looked different. They were all either sixth form girls or third form boys, that was partly it, but it was more the grouping and the tone that was striking. They were intermingled, but evenly, and they were chatting happily. Two girls with two boys led, the girls relaxed and the boys pleased with the attention; behind them a pair, and behind them another group of four, then more. There was something festive about the occasion as all these mixed groups, little families almost, set off somewhere as a special train. Unworthily, he wished he had a photo of it for the prospectus, because it reminded him of the photos they had tried to set up, but not quite managed – not like this. It was delightful.

He recognised Kate at the front of the procession. "Hullo. You all look pleased to be going wherever you're off to?"

Kate slowed and indicated the two boys with them. "These are our apprentices. We've all…" she nodded over her shoulder, "…just helped ourselves to one each from third form Latin, and now we're off to bake bread, aren't we, boys?"

"Apparently!" the nearer one made an unsuccessful attempt to look long-suffering.

Whitley smiled. "Well, good luck – I'm sure it will be a welcome break from conjugating irregular verbs." They swept on, and Whitley paused a moment to watch some more of them pass, and to breathe in their youthful spirit. How wonderful it all seemed.

Surprised and lifted by the encounter, he strode off to the workshops, where he noticed the mis-spelled sign for the first time. Still, with no prospect of visitors for a while he could ignore that now and pick them up on it later – or get Anthony to do it.

Four solid-looking boys were holding some chain and a tape measure to some sort of cushioned metalwork and a piece of wood. "This looks interesting," he said.

The boy with the tape – David Balfour, he thought – offered to explain. "It's a scrum-machine plough, sir. We've already got one working, but we thought a second would enable a bit of competition. The front end has come off the actual scrum-machine, then the chains go round the spreader," he indicated the piece of wood, "and that stops it narrowing on to the flankers, and then on to the plough behind – which we've got over there," he pointed into the depths of the workshop.

"Gosh," said Whitley, unable to think of anything more appreciative. "And you say there's a working model already?"

"Yes, sir – but that's being used by a so-called probable first team pack." He looked up from the machine to face up to the Head. "We aim to show that a so-called second team pack can take them in a straight race, furrow for furrow."

"Ah," nodded Whitley. "Well, you certainly have the determination – I'm sure you'll do it."

"Thank you, sir." David went back to his tape. Two of his fellows gave Whitley the sort of half-smile that said "nice of you to ask us but I expect you'll be going now".

"Jolly good," he concluded, wondering why they didn't simply use one of the tractors, and recognising young Barratt and Lyle, who were arguing about the difference between two files they were using on either end of some sort of metal tube. "And what have we here?"

Both boys jumped theatrically. "Oh! Hullo, sir."

"Seed-drill, sir."

"I see. How does it work?"

Barratt looked pained. "Well, it doesn't really, sir – at the moment."

Lyle intervened. "This tube goes under this funnel, you see, sir, and this..." he produced a piece of metalwork with some approximate welding on it, "is supposed to open and close this flap so that a seed only drops from the funnel when this wheel has completed a revolution." He paused to check he had the Head's understanding.

Whitley nodded encouragingly.

Barratt continued. "So you only get one seed every few inches..."

"The same distance apart as the circumference of the wheel, I expect..."

Barratt looked uncertainly at Lyle, who spoke for him. "That's right, sir."

"And the problem?"

Barratt took over again. "Oh, well, the flap's a bit wobbly and sometimes several seeds come out at once then it sticks and nothing comes out at all. It seemed easy when we designed it."

"I don't think we welded it very well."

"We thought if we got a really, really fast tractor we could just take the flap out altogether and the speed would make sure the seeds were spread out – what do you think, sir?"

Whitley faked a positive response. "Ah – a sort of e-type tractor? Good idea. Possibly a more expensive solution than fixing the flap, though?"

Barratt exhaled. "S'pose so," and got back to his filing.

Whitley drifted past boys using a power drill on a stand to spin what appeared to be a large circular lump of concrete on a conveyor belt that looked like a tank track. Beyond them a couple of lads seemed to be hitting pieces of grain with a hammer. A girl was doing something with what looked like a beautiful piece of silk. "I'm sure you could make something lovely with that," he said, rather lamely.

Emily looked up. "Yes, I'll get back to that – but now I'm just trying to see something else..."

"Oh – what?" Whitley encouraged.

Emily was tentative. "Well, you know when you harvest grain it's got chaff mixed in with it and you have to winnow it? We'll probably pour it out so it has to fall past a fan or something, but there may be no power, so I just wondered if I could do something with this silk. Maybe if you can drape it over the conveyor belt right, it'll catch the chaff and let the grain through, for instance. It's so delicate…"

"Good idea," said Whitley. He meant it. "Are the staff around at all? Mr Fry?"

Emily looked around. "I don't think Mr Fry's here, and Mr Adams went off with a couple of the boys to the Biology labs. Something to do with the insect farm…"

"The insect farm?"

"Most efficient way of producing nutritional matter, apparently."

Whitley's eyes opened wider. "You're going to have us eating insects?"

"If you're lucky. A delicacy in South east Asia, apparently. And someone said there was something about honey and locusts in the bible."

Whitley suspected she was right, but couldn't locate the reference in his head to inform her of it, so just nodded instead. "Well, I'll look forward to it. Good luck with the silk," he concluded. "Get as much as you can before someone eats the silk worms," he added. Emily smiled politely.

"I think Mr Smith and Gary are through there," she nodded towards a door. "But watch yourself," she cautioned somewhat cryptically.

Whitley opened the door quite slowly and popped his head around. A sixth former he recognised was working with a couple of younger boys, but no staff. "Hello, Miles."

Miles turned. "Oh, hello, sir."

Whitley took in the protective clothing, the slightly manic look of the younger boys, the awful look of a trough of sludge, and a rich but unpleasant smell. "What's going on here?"

"Sewage, sir – amazing stuff! You can burn off the gas, clean it and reuse it, make it into fertilizer or even just soil, and did you know you can even make a battery out of urine?" Miles waved his hand happily at various jars and containers. "I wish I hadn't given up Chemistry, but I suppose I can just study the interesting bits now – Mr Deacon is teaching me bits and pieces in house."

"Excellent, Miles – well done," said Whitley, backing out of the room. "I was just looking for Mr Smith?"

"I think he's in the annexe, sir – we've annexed the theatre. We ran out of room."

"Oh, I see. Thank you, Miles." On his way to the theatre, Whitley passed Rahman sitting at a particularly untidy-looking computer, wires and motherboards (or whatever they're called) everywhere, the green lines on the screen in odd patterns. "Rahman – you here too. How are you helping the communal effort?"

Rahman turned from the screen. "Sorry, sir?"

Whitley gestured around him. "Everyone seems involved in schemes to make us self-sufficient."

"Oh, yes, sir. Well, this – it's hard to say exactly what will come out of it. Maybe nothing. I mean originally I designed this game – you shoot aliens out of the sky." Whitley peered uncomprehendingly at the screen. "Well, they don't look like aliens – not that we know what aliens look like – but these blobs are aliens, and these lines at the side are guns, you see. Then watch." Rahman pressed a few keys, a line at the side of the screen moved a little, then a dotted line emitted from it, hitting a blob that then disappeared. Rahman grinned at the Head. "Pretty cool, eh, sir?"

Whitley raised his eyebrows and let them fall again. "Ur – yes."

"But then I got distracted. I mean actually I was wondering if I could give the aliens a way of shooting back, but that's not the point. I mean – do you know anything about computers, sir?"

Whitley shook his head. "No, not really – well, nothing at all, in fact."

Rahman pointed at all the wires and circuit boards and solder blobs that should have been neatly inside a box but didn't seem to fit. "Well all the actual computations go on in here, you see, and the keyboard just selects what's to be done. But the stored memory and capacity for unimaginably fast computing is all in there, and an interpretation of all that appears on here." He pointed to the screen. "So the product of everything going on in here, ends up going through there," he indicated a length of wire that attached the box to the screen. "Amazing, isn't it? Like your voice through the telephone wire, or the tv through an aerial."

"I see," said Whitley, seeing nothing, really.

"So," said Rahman, using the voice of a street corner magician, "what if the wire leading from a computer led to another computer?"

Whitley was utterly lost. "Indeed, yes – what if it could?"

Rahman initially spread his hands wide, indicating unlimited possibility, then turned them into a "search me" shrug. "Well, for one thing – the aliens could fight back! Not just as a machine programmed with set responses – you could have a friend on another computer acting for the aliens! How cool would that be?"

"Why not just play table tennis?" Whitley thought, but did not say. He didn't get it. "I have no idea how to scale cool," he said, "but I'm sure it would be very cool, as you say. Just don't spend too long on it."

"Oh, that's okay, sir – I've got as long as I need." Rahman returned to his machine, leaving Whitley uncertain that he'd made his point. Rahman was one of the school's best shots at an Oxbridge award for Maths or Physics, and his Headmaster would have been happier seeing him with a maths problem than behind a pile of wiring playing games in the workshops. Well, time enough for that when this crisis was over.

Re-emerging into the sunlight by the theatre, Whitley decided to skip the chaos that probably lay within it, and to go directly to seek out Tork. Despite his shoes and suit trousers, he cut through the scrub behind the two buildings and up to the road to head for the main course and the farm beyond. A purposeful walk proved just too brisk for the heat that awaited him beyond the trees, and to avoid the indignity of sweat he slowed as he approached the little drop to the farm buildings.

Suddenly the whole scene like a Brueghel painting appeared just below him. There by the red roll-tile roofs of the cluster of old stone-built barns and stables, Tork's reddish hair and tall, stringy frame marked him out in conversation with shorter, broader, darker Paul and a couple of white-shirted boys. In the shade of the walls could be seen the heads of a couple of cows standing in stalls, their milkers presumably at work, just out of sight. To the right, a duck pond, to the left, a long stretch of grasses bending slightly, the sweep of it interrupted by naked patches with loose bales sitting exposed in them, boys bending over some of them, urging them into shape. Others experimented with scythes. Passing into surrealism, eight boys in rugby kit packed down against a machine while a ninth fed the ball in before running around the back and hopping on to the plough to dig it into the ground. Rob Hackett, the master in charge of the 1st XV, hovered alongside, issuing instructions, tapping a shoulder here and a hip there, getting the boys parallel as the machine, the boy and the plough he stood on all moved forward across the bare patch to shouts and yells of effort and exhortation. Then it stopped, a dark line of new furrow behind it.

Whitley watched them a minute longer then allowed his eyes to track over each activity in turn. A boy with a scythe appeared to be practising a range of cricket shots with it. Two more had stopped and were lying down, apparently in minute examination of something on the ground. Maybe an ants' nest of possible protein. Two more seemed to be deciding on the best way to stack a few loose bales, and a group of three stood in a spot from which they could watch the sheep on the grass by the main drive. One boy, holding something away from his body, chased another. At the farm, two boys were apparently fixing some sort of reaping machine to the back of the three-wheeled mini bike or tractor, and another four were doing something at the edge of the duck pond that Whitley could not interpret. Beyond, the rolling countryside and farmland of the home counties stretched away, with no visible sign of the disease that was ravaging it.

The descent of the slope put the farm buildings in front of Tork and his companions for a while, but the group was still as it was when Whitley rounded the sun-soaked wall and arrived in their midst. "Morning, workers!" he greeted jovially.

"Headmaster – an unexpected pleasure," replied Tork.

"How's it going?"

Tork waved an arm towards the meadow of activity. "All busy," he said, "although we may be about to see the industrialization of the agricultural process..." he nodded towards the boys working on the tractor bike.

"Morning, Paul."

"Morning!"

Whitley finished his greetings with a nod to the boys.

"On a tour, Headmaster?" Tork asked.

"Yes, in a manner of speaking. I've just been to the workshops. Gather you're planning on feeding us insects?"

Tork nodded. "That's actually one of the most promising lines of enquiry, yes. The frog farm among the tadpoles there is another." Tork indicated the four boys in the duck pond.

"Or perhaps shooting aliens?"

Tork nodded again. "You met Rahman, then?"

"Yes. Bit concerned there actually – shouldn't we be making better use of him, or else leaving him to his Maths and Physics?"

Tork looked unimpressed. He shrugged. "The nature of research, Headmaster – you never know where things are going to spring from, so you research what's interesting, and find things that trigger other things. The best inventions are just that – things you hadn't expected or dreamed of. Otherwise it's just problem-solving – not that I've got anything against problem-solving, unless it wants to squeeze out invention, of course."

Paul had gone to see what the boys on the bike trailer were doing, and the others had gone to check on the duck pond. Whitley lowered his voice. "Are we going to be alright, do you think, Tork? How long can we last?"

Tork snorted half a laugh and looked at the ground. Then he looked up. "Have you heard that argument for the existence of a creator god? The one that charts all the incredible coincidences that were necessary to bring mankind about? Then concludes that the chances of our just happening are infinity to one, so it must have been planned by a god that made it happen?"

Whitley nodded. "Yes, yes – I know."

"Well, it starts from the wrong point, doesn't it? There may have been an infinity of different outcomes possible a few thousand years ago, but one of them had to happen, didn't it? And this one did. If I throw ten die down then no matter what combination comes up I can say that the odds against that particular result were astronomical, but you'd be unimpressed unless I'd first said that that particular result – and only that one - just had to be the one to come up. Our existence is only an incredible, against-all-odds outcome if you believe that we had to appear. But we didn't – almost anything else could have happened which didn't include us appearing, and it wouldn't have mattered: history would simply have gone another way. We don't really matter that much: we'll survive or we won't. No point worrying about it."

Whitley considered this. "But you're not really a fatalist – everything I've seen this morning shows you preparing to harvest crops next year and beyond."

"Yes, of course we are - I didn't mean you shouldn't prepare for the future – just that you can't control which one of an infinity of possible futures it's going to be. Harvesting our own crop is the future of the moment that we're in now, so prepare for that, but if the normal world suddenly comes back, and it's all change again – well, it's been fun, right? All this hasn't been a waste of time – even if it turns out it wasn't necessary - it was an experience." Whitley looked uncertain. "Okay, you think the normal world is coming back – fine. Think of it as a play you're watching. You know the play will end, but if you're thinking that, then you're missing the point of being at it. You have to be properly immersed in the play while it's happening. You have to be in the moment you're in. We're on our own and looking for ways to survive: we'll find them or we won't. Or something outside our control will save us – or bury us. Never mind that it's going to end – get on with the here and now of it."

Tork stopped and Whitley took his time, regarding him standing there in the sun of the moment. "I'll give you this," he looked again at the meadow of boys, and back over his shoulder to the school, then back to Tork. "I've enjoyed the school this morning. I've been worrying, it's true, but I've enjoyed the way the boys and girls are going about their lives this morning. I want this to end. I want this disease gone and my school and life as it was back, but when that happens, I'll try to remember your words: it's been fun, right?"

Tork smiled. "You're the man, Headmaster." He offered to high-five him, but he didn't seem to know what was going on, so he left it.

Whitley assumed a more brisk manner. "So what are these young chaps up to?" He strode off towards the nearest group of boys contemplating a few hay bales. Tork followed.

"Stooking up bales of hay, sir. There are different ways of doing it. And our bales aren't tied very tightly so that limits the options."

"Show me, if that's okay – Martin, is it?"

"Mark, sir – Mark Wright."

"Of course – Mark."

Mark leant two bales against one another. "They dry out best like this, sir," he held them in place and was clearly looking for a third. Whitley decided to pass him the one at his own feet. He stooped and his fingers slipped easily under the twine, so he lifted and swung it forward in the same motion. Immediately a fireball exploded in the small of his back before locking his entire spine solid in excruciating pain. He let out an agonised cry as the bale rolled forward and his arm dangled before him helplessly. He was wanting it to reach the ground and help him support the ton weight of red hot rock that the small of his back had become, but it wouldn't go. As he focussed on the distance between his hand and the ground he was desperate to lower it but couldn't make himself do it: the extreme pain in his back somehow, unimaginably but really, threatened to intensify further if he tried it. He howled, trapped between intolerable pain and the possibility of increasing it, helpless. He sensed the boys backing away as his knees sunk and he tried to stop his noise and manage the rest of the descent to the ground, but he couldn't over-rule some instinctive brake on his intentions. Then Tork's arm was below his chest and one of Tork's knees was on the ground in his field of vision, and his voice came through his own howl.

"Okay, Head, I've got you. I'm taking the weight and we're going down. Try to lie flat on the ground." Gradually the grass came up to meet him, his hands were on it and Tork was assisting him in a kind of reverse push-up. The pain plateaued. He was nearly there, his elbows fully bent, when it flared again, but pushing on his hands helped, then didn't, then made it worse, then as panic approached he happened to find a place that was almost tolerable. "Right – well done. Now we're going to turn you so you can lie on your back. Mark, come round this side of him with me – take his feet. Kyle, you go that side and help ease him down. Okay, are you ready, Head? You'll need to help us. One, two, three, go."

Tork rolled him over and other hands caught him as the sky appeared and shot across in front of him. He tried not to cry out. Mark had guided his feet over. The pain ran up and down his body like some fluid in a rocking vessel. He didn't know whether to try and arch his back or not. Tork's voice was sounding again. "You're best on your back. Take a moment. This is going to sound the craziest thing you ever heard but try to relax – the muscles will be in spasm going mad. Try to wind everything down, turn it off, don't tense."

"Don't tense!"

"Yup, I know, sounds mad, but try. Okay, boys, you did well. Back off, now, and give him some space."

Whitley lay staring at the clear sky as electric shocks ran up and down his back, trying to shut everything down. There didn't seem to be a position that didn't use muscles in the back. Sweat appeared on his brow. Tork's voice sounded again.

"Is this the first time you've done your back?"

"Nngh," he nodded.

Tork raised his voice. "Paul, we need a car to get him up that track and home, and he'll need painkillers before we can move him. Take the bike to sister in the san, ask her to drive here and bring a shot of morphine or something strong with her, okay?"

Paul nodded. "Bring car and morph – morphine?"

Tork nodded. "Car and painkiller – yes."

Paul put his helmet on while the boys made sure the trailer was clear, and then he was off. They heard the engine go up the slope and on to the surfaced road.

"Okay, lads, well done. Off you go – I'll call you when we need you." They went and Tork sat next to Whitley and looked into his ashen, sweating face. Whitley's eyes focussed on him. "Okay? Worst pain most guys go through, I'm told, but no-one dies from it. Sister will be here with a bit of relaxing painkiller soon, then we'll

130

get you off to lie on the floor at home, and you get a holiday. Is Mrs Linklater in, do you think?"

Whitley kept his eyes on Tork's, as if for comfort. "Should be. Nngh." Pain flashed.

"Good. She'll look after you." He saw the pain hit him. "It's bad, I know, but at least we don't have to do childbirth, eh?"

Tork wittered on and Whitley watched him and the sky. Sometimes the pain was almost okay, then it wasn't. He learned not to move, and to breathe. Eventually the car was heard, then voices. Sister's had the ring of professional concern and competence about it. They didn't want to take his jacket off, so she jabbed him in the side of the buttock through his trousers. Finally they laid him in the back of the car, by which time he was virtually delirious, and drove it slowly, with doors open, up the track then mercifully on to the tarmac. Someone had taken a stretcher to his house, and people got him out of the car and inside, and out of his jacket, and on to a thin mattress on the floor, while sister and his wife fussed around. Finally he was still and woozy, and everything was quiet.

Alison and Charles, apparently

Alison washed the flour and dough off her hands with excessive vigour, wondering how she'd somehow been demoted from a professional young teacher of maths to some domestic science assistant hanger-on trying to catch a husband. She stomped into the common room, ostensibly to check her pigeon-hole, but more because she really wasn't ready to go back to a house full of gossipy girls.

As normal in the late afternoon, especially since the withdrawal of tea and sandwiches, the common room was almost empty, and as luck would have it, the one person in there, just leaving through the far door, was Charles.

"Charles – *Charles*..." she hissed the repetition as he seemed not to hear her first summons. He paused his action of shutting the door behind him and looked back into the common room. His face lunged towards a happy smile then about-turned into a more concerned one as he registered more details of Alison's appearance. He came back in.

"Are you alright?" he asked.

"No," she flourished a poorly reproduced – via a banda machine – newsletter printed in purple. "Have you seen *this*?"

Charles raised his eyebrows. "*The Rag*, I assume." He produced a copy of his own from the handful of papers he was carrying. "I've had a quick look."

"At the 'Rumours' section?"

Charles attempted a dismissive expression that only betrayed that he had. "Just boys being boys: best to take no notice."

Alison snorted with derision. "That's so easy for you to say – you're not belittled by it."

Charles flinched. "Oh – thanks very much..."

She waved a hand in irritation at him. "I don't mean that. It's just – you have no idea what it's like being virtually the only female member of staff in what is still a boys' school, despite its recently having acquired a smattering of sixth form girls."

"No, I suppose not."

The pause seemed to make it inevitable that she would relent a little, so she read aloud instead. "Rumours that the mutual inspections of AL and CAM may lead to a bun in the oven are not half-baked." She glared at him.

He shrugged helplessly. "Just the usual nonsense..."

"It says you're going to make me pregnant!"

Charles flushed a little and cringed. "It's just innuendo – it's what they do. I mean it's a reference to the fact that you've started baking..."

"I have *not* started baking."

Charles flinched again. "You know what I mean – it just makes for an easy wordplay." He stopped unhappily.

She sighed. "Why did you make me do that inspection anyway?"

Charles waved his hands hopelessly. "I don't know – it seemed a fun thing to do. I was trying to be fun."

She looked at the list of editors and contributors on the newsletter. "Are any of these in your troop?"

"It could have been anyone – the boys at the gate may have told someone else, then they..."

She cut him off. "Yes, yes – but are any of these in your troop?"

Charles hesitated. "Tom Winters."

"Tom Winters? Do you think it may have been him?"

Charles looked troubled. "Why? What do you intend to do?"

"Do you think it may have been Tom Winters?"

Charles looked down. "Almost certainly. He more or less said he'd put something in."

"What?" Alison stared at him. He didn't repeat himself: she'd heard. "He said he would? And what did you say?"

Charles exhaled. "I really can't remember. We said something about free speech, censorship, inappropriate speculation... I don't remember exactly how it went."

"But you didn't tell him directly that he was not to print anything of this nature?"

Charles disliked being pinned wriggling in this way, but couldn't think of the way off. "You don't play things like this that way – look, a parent once told me I was to stand up in front of my form and tell them not to call his son 'jug-ears'. What would you have done?"

Alison was exacerbated. "What has that to do with anything?"

"I'm trying to stop you trying to do anything about what's in that wretched newspaper. Jug-ears outlived his nickname because I ignored his parents: if I'd done as they said then he'd have been jug-ears until the Upper Sixth, and probably beyond. If you want the rumour to die, then just ignore it." He sensed her weakening. "Worse things have been printed about staff, you know – just leave it." Suddenly she looked less like relenting and more like hitting him, so he searched desperately for another angle. "It's not really so belittling, you know, they think..."

"Oh, God, Charles, shut up!" He looked bewildered. She was too riled up to be able to explain properly. "These girls, they need to know they can choose what they want to be..."

Charles risked a snort. "Well, as for that, they're surprisingly traditional, aren't they? Getting a bloke and a bun in the oven is exactly what most of them want for themselves..." Alison went stone cold. Charles realised this had all just gone horribly wrong. "Sorry, I..."

"Just go."

"No, I didn't mean to imply...."

"Fine – if you're not going, then I will."

And she turned and left.

Tork ascendant

Elizabeth appeared in CDT. Chris was surprised but pleased. "Elizabeth! What a surprise: how nice to see you. Come to see how the other half lives?"

She flickered a token smile. "Looking for Tork, actually. Is he here?"

Chris indicated a door and started to move towards it. "In there with the sewage – perhaps I'd better get him for you?"

Elizabeth looked put out. "Ur – please," she said, and waited. Around her, various groups and individuals struggled on with all kinds of strange mechanisms and objects and tools. Others seemed to be drawing. Almost round the corner a boy at an apparently half-built computer suddenly yelled a "Hah!" noise. Boys near him stopped to watch as he leapt up, ran round his desk twice, punched the air, embraced one of them exuberantly, and sat back down again.

A cheerful third former caught her eye. "One of Rahman's breakthroughs," he explained.

"I see – thank you," she replied.

"You're welcome," he said, in what struck her as a stunning imitation of adult self-assurance.

Chris was bringing Tork to her in the manner of one displaying a prize exhibit. "Found him," he said, as if it were an achievement he hadn't been fully confident of managing.

"The Head has asked to see you – directly, if that's okay?"

"Of course – go – we're fine," Chris responded, as if he, as head of department, were the one being asked permission.

"How is he?" asked Tork as they walked towards the Head's house.

"As well as can be expected for someone immobile, drugged up to the eyeballs, and in pain anyway, I suppose." She looked up at him, conscious of his being tall, and somehow made her eyelashes noticeable. "Apparently you were really good with him – he's full of praise for the way you handled it, or him."

Tork looked back. "Good of him to say so."

"I think you made an impression."

There seemed nothing to be done with this remark, so Tork simply let it go. They walked on. "He's not trying to work is he? Is Brick there to take over and get him to stand down?"

"Ian's not there, no."

"Oh."

They turned off out of the sun and down the tree-lined avenue that led to the Head's house. Jenny Linklater, standing by the front door, saw them approaching, gave a little wave, and went in, presumably to relay the news that they were on their way. She reappeared just as they were arriving.

"Hello, Tork – thanks for coming." It was a formal greeting: they didn't really know each other. "Well done, Elizabeth. Come in, come in," she showed the way, "he's in the sitting room. Will you take some coffee, tea? Perhaps some squash – such a hot day?"

"I'm fine, thanks." He walked past her and hesitated while she shut the inner door behind them and then led the way to Whitley, sitting bolt upright on a hard chair, his hands pressed down on the seat either side of him, his feet up on a chair before him, his brow sweating.

"Thanks for coming, Tork."

"Headmaster – shouldn't you be laying flat?"

"In a minute – I just need to do this first."

Tork registered surprise but also acceptance with his facial expression. "Well," Jenny said, "I'll leave you to it." She faced Whitley as she backed out. "Just yell if you need me." Whitley gave a tight nod and she disappeared, closing the door noiselessly.

"Take a seat." Elizabeth sat in an armchair a little to the side. Another armchair facing Whitley on the far side of the room seemed a long way away, and Tork helped himself to a nearby hard chair instead, placing it by Whitley in a manner that felt more like visiting a hospital bed.

"How are you doing?"

Another tight nod. "I've been better, but sister seems fairly confident that it's a straightforward case of pain management and immobility for a week or two. She's adamant, however, that I won't be able to concentrate, should avoid stress," he gave a slight roll of the eyes that Tork acknowledged with a little lift of the head, "and that I'm liable to make mistakes as well as delay recovery if I try and do anything other than rest."

Tork nodded. "I'm sure she's right. Brick can manage."

Whitley took a moment, busying himself with a wave of pain, then replied. "Ian is indeed a brick, as his nickname implies. It also has other, more mischievous, quite unjustified implications. He's an excellent number two." He rolled his eyes over from the contemplation of pain to Tork's face. "But is an excellent number two what is needed in such extraordinary times?"

Tork shrugged. "Number one would have been better, but we'll manage."

Whitley gave the tiniest shake of the head: he didn't really have the strength to go through all this. "He'll cling to routines, stick to standing orders – delay decisions. Wait until the boss is back." He closed his eyes. "No. I can't rest here knowing that he's at the helm while we are navigating these particular waters." His eyes opened and he looked straight at Tork. "He's a good man. Anything, anything at all with normal routine, with keeping life as normal going, ticking over, you leave it to him." The ambiguity of that "you" rang around Tork's head. "But as for getting us through this crisis – I need you to do that."

Tork shook his head a little, shrugged. "I'm doing all I can, happy to carry on..."

Whitley held his hand up and breathed, then spoke. "It has to be as headmaster. Otherwise it'll come back here – Tork wants to do this but Ian says no..." he shook his head. "We need you to do this, Tork." Tork looked dazedly at Elizabeth, who began a reassuring smile, but Tork had already looked back to Whitley, who was still speaking, but more quietly. "Start tonight at the housemasters' meeting. Be acting headmaster. I've seen you run a housemasters' meeting: you'll be fine."

"They won't believe it."

"Elizabeth will confirm, as will Ian."

"Ian?"

Whitley was fading. "I've already seen him."

Tork was taken aback a second. "What did he say?"

Whitley smiled faintly. "He'll need a minute, but he'll be there tonight, your loyal number two." It was all wrapped up. Tork didn't have a choice. "Thank you, Tork. Good luck. Could you possibly call Jenny and help me down? I need to try to sleep."

Minutes later, Whitley nearly asleep on a mattress on the floor, Jenny and Elizabeth fussing, Tork stepped out of the Head's house, Acting Headmaster, Brambling College. He put his face up to the bit of sun that snuck through the leafy trees. He wanted to go and see Eve, but hadn't time, really. Instead, he exhaled heavily, and, directing his gaze to the path back to school, he muttered quietly.

"Didn't see that coming."

Supper

"I reckon it's rat," Barratt speculated to Lyle about the odd-looking stew that had been delivered to his plate beside a lump of homemade bread.

"Sewer rat, probably," Lyle replied as the two of them headed off to find a space at a table.

The snippet of conversation landed on Tork's shoulders as the boys passed, and he paused from eating to contemplate it. He hadn't thought of rats. Didn't they say there was always one within three yards of you? Must be millions on the estate.

It was odd sitting in the dining hall with all the staff, boys and girls, the only one who knew that he was their headmaster, or would be by tonight.

Mike sat down with his tray. "Evening, all. Heard about the head?"

Charles looked up. "No. What?"

"Out of it, apparently. Totally poleaxed by back trouble. Back at base, drugged up and off with the fairies. Pass the salt." He looked at his plate. "Anyone know what it is?"

"Gosh – poor chap."

"Well, Tork will know about it," Mike looked expectantly at him, "it happened on the farm, apparently."

Tork nodded. "Hay bale. Classic bad lift. We had to send Paul off to the san for sister, car and painkillers."

"So that's Brick in charge," Mike contemplated. The observation needed no answer, so Tork didn't give one.

Charles had spotted Alison. He put the rest of his piece of bread down. "I wonder if there's any jam left? Only civilised to have a spot of pudding." He picked up his plate and bread and stepped over the bench to go and see.

Tork finished his supper and looked up to see James and Charlie two tables away, startled to have found themselves suddenly meeting his eyes. It looked as if they were talking about him.

"Gotta go," Tork explained as he left.

Mike nodded. "Cheers."

Charles joined Alison looking through the wreck of the sauce and accompaniment offerings.

"Evening."

She jumped a little, but her voice was even. "Good evening."

Charles glanced around a little. "Look, I'm sorry if..."

She cut him off icily. "You think it's a good idea to have a personal conversation here, in front of the whole school?"

Charles hadn't really anticipated a personal conversation: he thought a quick apology could have been followed up with a bit of small talk and the air cleared. But it was no good trying to say so: she had already left.

The Assumption

Although he had decided that no work up there was necessary tonight, Tork had ended up on the roof anyway. The sun was yet to set. It hovered low and golden, just beginning to suggest a hint of red that could streak the sky. Tork looked east to the tallest garden monument, a pillar from the very top of which a roman emperor with the face (apparently) of one of Brambling's early dukes, lit by the sun from below, oversaw the growth of the estate, surveying smugly the imposing of classicism on the English countryside. On the main house roof, Tork was actually higher still, and winked at him across the chasm between them. Then he looked further away at the Gothic Temple, and imagined Eve and Dylan at home in the woods beyond it. It had been Eve who had told him about the emperor's face being a likeness of the Brambling Duke, History being her bag, not his.

King of all he surveyed, he felt both powerful and oddly inadequate, as if this day were ending less well than the one before it had done. He wandered aimlessly along the roof, and stopped to watch the cattle in the Grecian Valley, grazing between the trees. Leaders knew about History, didn't they? Not just snippets they'd picked up from their wives or bits of facts imaginatively reworked in plays and radical fiction, but directly.

The cows stood as still as the air, nothing whispered through the trees, no insect hummed. A single bleat echoed from an arrangement of sheep on the parkland. The western sky turned redder as the sun sank lower. Darkness that had clung to the trees sagged and seeped out. The sun ceased expanding and lost its shape as it dipped through the thicker atmosphere and most of the way below the horizon, leaving just the top of its head, a red light lingering a second longer. Tork understood the significance of the way the duke's monument had been placed as the whole of the estate was engulfed in a shadow that then climbed his pedestal:

142

above the darkness, the duke in his roman emperor's clothes stood alone in the sunlight, radiant above the gloom, basking in his moment of splendour.

Then he, too, was immersed, and as Tork watched his eclipse, he sensed the continuing warmth on the back of his own head. Turning, he realised that his own face was still in the sun, and that it was he who must now be standing solitarily resplendent, his hair on fire, in the unearthly incandescence of his own moment in a celestial spotlight above the blackout below.

He closed his eyes and felt the air suddenly cool on his face, although warmth still pulsed from the lead on the roof. When he opened them again, night had begun.

He sat down and gazed toward the darkened duke. Heads verbalised a strategy, a plan, a vision of the future at their first meeting in charge, didn't they? The imminent housemasters' meeting gave him the butterflies of pre-performance, except that he'd just discovered that it wasn't impro, there were lines to be learned after all, and he didn't know them.

The moon had risen by the time he stirred himself, but as he neared the hatch door that would take him back into the mansion he noticed the thermal still working off the heated south front façade below. The lichen his hand knocked off the roof balustrade fell up into the air. He wondered if some sort of flying suit with an integral wing could support him long enough to fall from here into the lake, about a quarter mile away. Actually it was probably further than that. So probably not.

He needed a prompt, that was the trouble. If some colleague or parent was spouting reactionary nonsense about education to him, he would respond fluently and lengthily with his own view of education, just bang, rising from the moment, the characters, the context, here it is… But to approach a sober, probably stunned housemasters' meeting with a prepared statement of actual intent was quite different. He needed air under his wings, the charge of interchange, not a standing start.

Nietzsche was in his basket but Elizabeth didn't seem to be in her room. Hearing a noise in the Headmaster's office – in *his* office – he peered around the door. Elizabeth was closing shutters and curtains.

"Good evening, Headmaster," she smiled.

Tork puffed his cheeks out briefly, let his eyebrows leap. "I think it would take a lot longer than a recovery from a back injury for me to get used to being called that."

"Oh, you'd be surprised – I've left the minutes of the last meeting on your desk," she indicated the head's desk in the corner. He strolled over. Tried the unexceptional chair. Glanced at the minutes – a written record of a meeting he'd attended himself only yesterday, so no surprises there. He looked up. Spinning round from the final window briskly, Elizabeth's movement made her skirt flare, bunch on one side, and fall back on the other.

"Is that skirt pleated?" Tork asked.

Elizabeth, pleased, looked down. "Yes – do you like it? It's nice to wear something loose and airy in the hot weather."

Tork looked at the skirt a moment longer. "It's just that a girl in Design was wanting to make a pleated skirt from silk. I didn't know if it would work."

"Oh, I don't suppose this is real silk..."

"No."

The outer door opened and closed. Then Brick came in. "Good evening, Headmaster," he said.

Tork grinned. "Thank you, Ian – although in truth I think that's more your role. I'm a sort of temporary emergency chief executive, I think – perhaps the harbour pilot to your ship's captain."

Brick visibly warmed. Elizabeth purred. Tork inwardly gawped. He must have written that line on the roof, but he had no memory of doing so. Blimey, he was good at this.

Brick produced a piece of paper. "I've got a few things I thought we should go over in the meeting – would you care for a look?" He handed over what appeared to be some very tedious details about changes to channels of communication and everyday routines. "Just housekeeping stuff – do you want me to take you through them in advance?"

Tork gave them back. "That's alright – perhaps if you would take us all through them together?"

Brick took the list back. "Of course." He paused. Tork attempted to look receptive to any further suggestions. "I don't know if you've had time to give much thought to the announcement of the new arrangement?" Tork shook his head a little and gestured uncertainty. "It's just that unless you have something specific prepared, I was just going to offer – I'd be very happy to introduce you as Headmaster, if that would help. They'll be expecting me to take charge of the meeting. I could do so, just for long enough to hand over to you."

Tork stepped forward and grasped Brick's hand. "Thank you, Ian – thank you."

The housemasters sat through the meeting far more quietly than usual, and it really seemed they couldn't wait to get away. From the moment Brick announced the new arrangement they lacked focus – not that Brick's list was exactly engaging anyway, and Tork, faced with such an audience, had little to add. Ironically, all Tork had really said was "as you were".

The meeting ended quite quickly, and they all filed out. Roger stepped out of the queue for the door and shook Tork's hand. "Congratulations," he said, before quickly resuming his place in the shuffle to the door. Simon, behind him, obviously considered following suit, but smiled instead.

"And good luck," he said.

Philip gestured to Elizabeth, was she walking home, should he wait. She shook her head: not sure how long to finish up – you go.

He went to catch up Deborah. More half smiles and nods to the Brick, Elizabeth, Tork trio as the others left.

"Well," said Brick as the outer door closed, "that went okay, didn't it?"

Tork and Elizabeth exchanged a glance, nodded. "Seemed fine," she said.

"I wonder what they think?" Tork shook his head to show he wasn't really asking.

Brick smiled and looked at the doorway. "They think if not me then surely one of them." He switched his look to Tork. "But they'd tear themselves apart trying to decide *which* one." He put a hand on Tork's shoulder. "Just keep doing what you were doing anyway, and let me handle them." He took his hand away and patted his pockets, as if checking them. "I'll leave you to it, if that's okay?"

Tork nodded. "Thanks, again, Ian," he said, as Brick left the room.

"Good night, gentlemen," they heard him say in the corridor.

Tork looked a moment longer at the door through which Brick had made his exit. "What a great guy – I had no idea."

Elizabeth nodded. Then she pointed at her notebook. "We usually just check what I'm going to minute?"

"Oh, of course."

"Perhaps if you just sit at your desk?"

Tork complied mindlessly. A swell of chat arose and a burst of laughter erupted in the corridor. As it ebbed, Roger's voice suddenly stood out, "the trick was obviously to pick one that the governors couldn't possible decide they preferred!" and the laughter swept back.

Elizabeth had gone. Tork heard the outer door burst open. "We *can* hear every word you're saying in there," the last word came with bitter scorn, "*gent*lemen!" Tork expected her to reappear, but

146

she didn't. She must have been standing there, glaring, as the assembly slunk off.

An unidentifiable voice ventured "'Night, Elizabeth," but there was no reply.

She came back with a flush on her cheek. "Sorry about that – bloody idiots."

Tork raised both his hands. "Please don't apologise – you were magnificent." He waited for her adrenaline rush to settle a little. "Thank you, Elizabeth. I mean I know it was as much a point of general decorum as a defence of me personally, but I'm still touched – thank you. And you were tremendous: I wish I could have seen it." He smiled.

She blew out through closed lips and smoothed her palms on her skirt over her hips. "Haven't done anything like that in quite a while," she said. She found her notebook, smoothed her hair off her forehead, and came forward to the desk, placing the notes in front of him for his inspection. He looked at them and, alarmed, looked up at her. "Sorry," she said, "I use Pitman's shorthand and get pretty well everything. That way you can just tell me which bits not to bother with and I cross them out before I type them up. He looked back down at the notes and she stood beside his chair and bent forward to point to where she was reading with her left hand, a pen poised in her right. "So this bit is just date, time, title, apologies from WL, all else present, IBM opened the meeting explaining the situation re WL's back injury..." He sensed the slight flutter in her body, post confrontation. She faltered. "Sorry, is this alright? I could just type it all up and you could go through it more easily crossing things out yourself?"

"No, no," reassured Tork, "it's fine – whatever you usually do."

She'd moved away slightly, but now returned and made to continue. "There had been no visit from the doctor, of course, but sister seemed confident that after two weeks' absence he should be able to gradually..." she trailed away again. "I suppose there's no real reason why you have to see the notes – am I crowding you?"

"No, no," reassured Tork again, "it's fine – in fact, I like it."

In the stillness of the moment, her body simply failed to move away, but it felt as if she'd moved towards him. There was a tensing in her neck as she turned her head a few degrees from the notes to face him. Then he was shocked to realise he'd experimentally slipped his tongue into her mouth.

Her response was so willing and enthusiastic that after a short while it seemed rude not to slide his hand up her leg beneath the aforementioned loose pleated almost silk skirt, so he did so, and was assailed by a cocktail of emotional and intellectual reactions on discovering stocking tops, a suspender, bare skin. He didn't think anyone dressed like that anymore.

A few breathless moments later, he thought he'd clearly gone too far when she pulled away, but instead of a slap or intensely awkward moment, she simply made some minor adjustment, touched her toes briefly, then sent cascades dancing through the hem of her skirt as her left knee lifted itself. Then in a single motion as elegant as ballet, a pointed toe passed over his lap and her body twisted and flowed after it until she stood astride him. The skirt seemed decorously to cover her hands as she undid his trousers, extracted his member, and lowered herself on to it. Tork had leaned back and automatically assisted her efforts. Awash on the unexpected physical sensation of what she was doing to him, an extraneous concern about the mechanics of the operation to follow occurred to him. He'd never had sex on an upright chair. He wondered if he should move his feet to be better able to play his part, but then realised that his part was in its final act anyway.

Opening his eyes soon after to see through Elizabeth's hair and over her shoulder the office of the Headmaster, windows shuttered, housemasters' chairs in a circle, the thought arrived from nowhere, "so this is power." And as she shifted and his already shrunken machismo fell in his lap, he wondered if he was really equipped for it.

Elizabeth did the reverse ballet step and her skirt fell automatically into place: she looked immaculate. "Goodness," she said, "where did that come from?" She smiled and stooped quickly. "I expect that will be all for tonight?"

Her panties balled tightly in one hand, she scooped up her notebook in the other, smiled and left. She quickly visited the ladies visitors' loo across the corridor, came back to fetch Nietzsche, and left her office a second time, calling "'Night!" as she left.

Walking back through chapel court, a little too briskly for Nietzsche, she smiled to herself. The sex had been okay: Tork was really quite sweet. And that made two out of three Headmasters. But best of all would be the delicious thrill of seeing the enviously titillated moral outrage on Deborah's face.

Tork, meanwhile, had rerun a few times that reverse ballet step, the swish like stage curtains announcing the end of the show as her skirt resumed, how immaculate she looked as she delivered her lines, "Goodness, where did that come from? I expect that will be all for tonight?" Then, it was the next bit, really. As she had scooped up her notebook, and he had sat there with his trousers humiliatingly open, he had been disappointed she didn't look more dishevelled. And he felt like he'd just had his bottom wiped by his mum.

Part Four

Szlachta revisited

Chelmsford Charlie ran a couple of steps to catch James. "So she's the headmaster's wife now – the lady of the manor."

"I suppose so."

"Do you think she'll still help us?" Charlie reshuffled the armful of books that he was taking to morning school – three lessons before break, all of which seemed likely to be taught.

James, who only had his English lesson before a session with a reed-harvesting team, thought about this. "I don't know. It's difficult to imagine her moving into the Head's house and all that. I can't imagine her anywhere but there, really."

Charlie took this as reassurance initially, then wondered if it reflected more on James's imagination than on likely developments. "Still, we've got that book she leant us. I could probably do my history project on my own now. It was just good to have her to ask questions." It was also just nice to go there, have tea and chat, even play with Adds, Charlie thought, but did not say. He'd enjoyed their visits, and was pleased James had shared his discovery of her with him, although he still didn't know what to think about his having half-said, and then withdrawn, that the first time he saw her she had been naked.

"Glad all that work has done something for someone," James muttered, "Floozy Parker seems to have forgotten about it."

"You're so utilitarian, serf." James didn't bother replying, or pointing out that he only knew half the words Charlie had used. "Ah," Charlie noticed they had arrived, literally, at the perfect metaphor for his friendly insult, "and here we are at the parting of the ways: I'm off to three lessons of enlightenment, you to a single lesson of basic English then out to the fields." He turned off for Maths, leaving James headed for English.

150

Thirty minutes later it was obvious to Mr Parker that the rather stimulating discussion he'd felt sure would have been generated by his astute comparisons of their present situation with Chaucer's Middle England was simply not going to fly. He was, as ever, disappointed. He really had thought there was a chance of his being excited by the insights of his charges, and, of course, the resultant opportunities to be even more insightful himself in reply. He again wondered how he could convince Simon Harker, or Boozey Harker as the Head of English was apparently known, to give him top sets only. He was wasted on the likes of 3C.

Unable to stand any longer the plodding efforts of his class to try and get as far as the point that had, in fact, been his starting point for this discussion, Parker held his hand up for silence. He considered summing up, but there was nothing to add to what he'd said, and they had failed to understand, at the start of the lesson. The school's unwitting re-enactment of some medieval mores would have to remain unexamined and unappreciated. But that left ten minutes to go. His eyes fell on James Redmund.

"James, weren't you going to tell us about the fruits of your research?" Parker would have to be careful, he supposed, not to spend the whole of the last ten minutes amusing the class with a comically caustic reduction of James's blundering efforts – he was a perfectly nice lad, after all, just a bit of a fool. Still, this could sort out a bit of unfinished business and use up at least some of the time.

James got hesitatingly to his feet. "Ur, yes, sir. Szlachta, sir. It actually turned out to be quite interesting..." He looked around him. They didn't look convinced, although they were intrigued that he had actually claimed to have some sort of personal response to an academic exercise.

To everyone's surprise, including his own, James then spoke for nine minutes uninterrupted, and sat down to the kind of general, but essentially polite, applause that the class gave a full, formal spoken English exercise such as a talk on 'my hobby' or a debating speech on school uniform. Mr Parker was stunned.

Eventually he lifted his chin and looked around so the class knew to stop applauding and allow him to speak. "Well, thank you, James, I must say – that was excellent. Really quite fascinating, and delivered with enthusiasm, and even some modest rhetorical skill. In fact, much better than, as far as I remember, your actual class talk. Perhaps I should revise the mark. I particularly liked the way you brought in Joseph Conrad and the onboard society of the ship. But perhaps you knew I was a particular fan of Joseph Conrad?" James, who had no idea who Joseph Conrad was, other than someone Eve had told him about, simply smiled in the sunshine of high regard, which Parker took as silent confirmation of his cunning currying-favour theory. "Aha. But even though I've caught you in your ruse, it's still effective. Well done." Parker continued to regard James: there was something else, wasn't there? "Even though," he added, "we never really got to the bottom of the *context*," he put the word in highlights and underlined it, "did we?"

James furrowed his brow. "It was something Mr Fry said, sir. Something about the way we do things becoming szlachta-like, and when that happened, Brambling would be ready."

With less than a minute of the lesson to go, the class was intrigued, but also a little exasperated, to notice that Mr Parker suddenly seemed to be going in slow motion. "Mr Fry said that?"

"Yes, sir."

"And when, exactly, was this?"

James exhaled and looked about him for help. "I don't know exactly, sir – it was ages ago now."

"But was it *before* we closed off the school?"

He seemed worryingly intense about this irrelevant detail. His classmates seemed already to have forgotten James's triumph and were growing annoyed by his delaying the end of the lesson. James remembered Eve knowing what szlachta was, then the CCF soldiers in their truck, and running back to the house announcement.

"Yes, sir – definitely before that."

For a moment, Mr Parker remained motionless.

"Class dismissed," he eventually said.

The Admirable Crichton

Tork had had a good morning on the farm and in the workshops, and the fending off of all the comments and questions about how his new post would change him had been part of the fun, really. Elizabeth had greeted him with, perhaps, a more than usually warm and full smile, but otherwise made no reference to the previous night, simply asking when he would be free to see any of the people who would inevitably come and ask for an appointment. As good as his word, he arrived back at the Head's office during morning break. Elizabeth said she'd managed to put most of them off, although Philip and Ian both insisted they needed to see him before the housemasters' meeting, but she wondered if he wanted to see the student journalists.

"What student journalists?"

Elizabeth consulted her notes. "Tom Winters of *The Rag* and Hugh Merrill of *The Brambling News.*"

"Okay, when?"

"Ten minutes. Do you want a preview of their questions?" she handed him a handwritten sheet.

He gave them a quick look. "I might just get a cup of coffee." He was drifting towards the door.

"Okay – you can nip into the common room or I can just make you one here, if you like."

Tork turned to the cups and coffee machine in the corner. "Oh, of course." He hesitated. "Actually, perhaps I should just put my head in the common room?"

She smiled. "As you wish. The boys will arrive in ten minutes: they can wait here for you."

Roger was just coming out of the common room as Tork entered.

"'Morning, Roger."

"'Morning, Tork."

Still looking at his sheet of paper, Tork paused. "Actually, Roger?"

They turned to face each other.

"Yes?"

"What's this *Brambling News*?"

Roger looked at the sheet of paper, then realised he didn't need to. "Oh, that's the official version being set up to put *The Rag* out of business."

"And will it?"

Roger dismissed the idea. "Hardly – which would you read? An actual salacious, scurrilous student newspaper produced by actual scurrilous, salacious, probably scabrous students, or a supervised, bowdlerised, school PR version?"

Tork nodded. "Take your point – thanks."

He proceeded down the corridor, realised he probably wasn't even expected to look at his pigeon-hole because surely Elizabeth would do that for him, and headed for the coffee. Alison was just putting her cup back.

"How's it going shooting boys in the shadows?" he asked.

She put the cup down. "I'm surprised you even remember that, given everything that's happened since." Tork filled his own cup. "Yes, it works well, thanks, although I haven't really used it the way we designed yet. I expect you'll be too busy now if I do need a photo taking off it."

Tork looked genuinely surprised. "No – not at all. Bring it anytime."

Alison chose not to point out that she could walk all the way down there and he'd probably be nowhere to be found. "Actually, I could do with a word sometime."

"Now?"

She shook her head. "I'm teaching. I'll track you down later."

She went. Tork remained drinking his coffee as the rest of the room emptied, smiling hello to him as they passed to get back to lessons. Mike risked a joke as he walked by. "Alright for some, eh? I guess you can take your time getting to lessons now…" Tork smiled with his mouth, but not his eyes. Mike felt a flush of humiliation as he continued on his way. Stupid remark. Tork had never worried about being on time for lessons anyway.

Back in Elizabeth's office, Tork sat and faced the two boys. "So this is a bit of a face-off? *The Rag* versus *The Brambling News*?"

Both boys looked uncertain. "I guess so," said Tom.

"No," said Hugh, at exactly the same moment. "We thought it would be better for you – that you'd be more likely to agree to do it – if you could do both of us at once."

Tork held up the questions. "Look, guys, I'll level with you. I can find the time. But these questions are so awful, I can't summon up the interest." They both looked a bit crushed. "Some of these questions just ask me to respond with a prepared 'Head's PR' statement – good for a prospectus, lousy for a student newspaper, boring for the three of us – and others directly ask for behind the scenes information I'm obviously not going to give – even if I knew it." He paused. They looked at him. "It's probably pretty obvious who wrote which?" They half-smiled uncertainly. "If the idea is to get some sort of personal insight into the acting head, then don't interview the post, interview the person. You know who I am – think what to ask. You can have one question each, when you're ready."

He got up and went to Elizabeth's desk. "Can you send them in when they're ready?"

"Yes, of course."

"And can you look up for me who those guys were who got busted about a term ago for trying to brew their own beer? Is that alright? I'd like to see them afterwards, if you can manage it."

"Okay," she got up and headed for some box-files.

"Should be on your computer, really…" he said lightly as he went next door.

There didn't seem to be anything in his office that needed doing. Elizabeth had apparently protected him so well from work that there was nothing to do but gaze out of the window down the south front and wait for the journalists. They weren't long.

He sat at his desk and let them sit opposite him. "Okay, what have you got?"

Hugh began. "Which would you say was really your subject, Design or Drama?"

Tork steepled his fingers, nodded, and looked back at him. "Okay – good question. Although I don't think I'm going to give it a direct answer. I started in stage design – building play sets – so both, really. Why should anyone have only one 'real' subject? Are the differences between subjects real?" He sat forward. "You have something – an observation about the world – that you want to think about. Then it gives you an idea, that becomes a plan – perhaps a drawing, a script, an hypothesis. You work on it. Suddenly it's a rehearsal, an experiment, a working model, and then it's a theory you offer up for peer review, a play you give to an audience, a product you deliver to a consumer. And that interaction between your developed idea and a world of people is – well, life." He spread his hands. "All proper subjects are pretty much the same. Next."

It had all gone a bit fast. Tom realised he was being asked for his question. "Oh, ur – what's your favourite play?"

"Ah," Tork changed his position and chortled a little. "This is beginning to look as if I've already lost the capacity to give a straight answer, but your favourite play tends to be the one you're working on. As it should be – I'm not sure you've any right to impose on your cast, crew and audience unless you think it's for the best thing you've ever done."

"So what are you working on?"

Tork gave a 'nice try but no' smile. "It's not for public announcement yet."

"But you are working on one?"

"Always."

Tom looked thoughtful. He needed to try again somehow. "But is it a scripted play or one of your impro-based progressive ones?"

Tork laughed at the description. "Yes, I guess you could call it an impro-based progressive one."

"So if you're not working on a playscript, you could choose a favourite?"

Tork nodded. "Nice. You got me. *The Admirable Crichton*."

Tom jumped a little with surprise and desire to know what exactly to write down. "The Admiral...?"

"Admirable. Crichton."

"How do you spell that?"

"C-R-I-C-H-T-O-N."

"And it's your all-time favourite play?"

Tork sat back. "No, I don't think so. I don't really do 'my top five' stuff. *The Admirable Crichton* just popped into my head, but I'd be surprised to be told it's my favourite play. I like it, but I think I hate that it's going to go down in black and white as my favourite play, but I don't know what is, and you insisted on an answer, so I guess I'm stuck with it." The three of them looked at one another for a moment. "Okay, are we finished?"

The boys got up. "Yes, sir. Thank you, sir."

Philip had somehow divined that Tork was free, and was right there while Elizabeth asked Hugh, who was going to the Art School, to send Gerry Horsham and Tadhg O'Donelly back. Philip didn't seem to require any opinions or decisions from Tork, he simply seemed to need to tell him what he'd been doing and what he hoped to do soon. Tork said 'good' and 'well done' and 'okay' a lot, then swapped Philip for Gerry and Tadhg.

"Sir?" They announced themselves.

"Thanks for coming," Tork started. "You two brew beer." Tadhg looked down and Gerry glared. "Right?" Nothing. "Well you did at least once – so did you just stop?" A look of pure contempt came over Gerry's face, and he seemed to be squaring up, in a neanderthal sort of way. Tork looked straight at him, "What?"

Gerry sneered then tutted. "You've changed already – on your first morning. Trying to catch us out. Since when were you one for the petty oppression of some minor rule-breaking? It's gone to your head, sir."

Tork sighed. "I'm looking for someone who can brew beer."

"Right." Stated with all the knowing cynicism of youth.

"So?" Tork prompted hopefully.

Gerry shifted his stance, swapped a look with Tadhg. "We had a go last summer holidays, didn't we, Tag?"

"Holidays, yea. And that one other time, but we didn't finish that batch. It got confiscated." They looked accusingly at Tork, who was clearly now on the side of the prohibitionists. Beer. You were either for it or against it.

"How long does your process take?"

Gerry narrowed his eyes with low cunning. "Less than the length of the summer holidays," he said, catching Tadhg's eye, both pleased with his neat evasion of Tork's trap.

Tork shook his head resignedly. "Look guys, I thought we could spit roast a few sheep over open fires along the south front for a kind of barbecue supper one evening, okay?" They looked at him guardedly. "And I thought it would be nice, for staff and the sixth form at least, to have a beer with it. Sounds good, eh?" But the boys still gave nothing away. "So I was wondering if we could supplement whatever beer we've got left in store, and I also thought how appropriate it would be if we could offer a bit of home brew – see?" It really wasn't clear if they saw or not. "We've been moving towards self-sufficiency, so the home-brew would just complete the scene: self-baked bread, mutton roasting on open fires, self-brewed beer..." The boys, street-wise mice, saw only the compelling red-haired python trying to draw them in. He changed strategy. "Hello?" he clicked his fingers in front of them, but they reacted badly to the sarcasm they so often enjoyed, flinching and drawing back. Tork more or less gave up. "Think about it, okay? If the time comes when you hear there's going to be a spit-roast barbecue instead of the usual supper arrangements one night, then perhaps you might pop in to see Miss Banks next door and let her know that you've 'found' some home-brew and will be bringing it along. Then I can write you a note for the caterer to supply you with whatever yeast, grain, help you need for the next batch – okay?"

Nothing.

"Good chatting with you. Off you go."

They retired. Tork stared at the door they closed behind them.

Heraclitus revisited

Tom, hesitating outside the Head's offices, had watched Hugh go off to the Art School with his message for Gerry and Tadhg. He thought about the interview: it would be good if *The Rag* got further than *The Brambling News* on this one. Same interview, but an interesting article on it in the original paper, and a rubbish one in the new one – that would be a really good result. Take that, *Brambling News*. It would help too if he got more out of his 'favourite play' question than either of them got from Hugh's 'favourite subject' one. He looked again at his notes. *The Admirable Crichton*. He thought about it. Maybe they had it in the library, or, better still, some sort of quick summary of it. He climbed the stairs.

Heraclitus was gazing out of the windows at the magnificent summer. Summers always have their attractive associations, although they change with age. Recently, in the librarian phase of his life, he'd enjoyed the way the boys and girls started nesting in the library in summer. Deciding there were 'too many distractions' in their own studies, and exams nearing, some started using the library instead, quickly selecting a favourite spot then gradually, unconsciously, furnishing it with pens, jumpers, good luck charms, postcards – probably precisely the distractions they had come to avoid in the first place. They tended to leave them all in place as they just 'nipped out'. He was supposed to discourage it, lest the workspaces effectively 'bagged' by the possessions of absent students became so numerous as to deny sufficient spaces to those present. But that was never actually going to happen. He occasionally indicated a messy desk to its 'owner', and they were always polite: "Sorry, sir – I'll tidy it up in a minute, if that's okay," and they meant to, but they didn't.

Besides nesting upper sixth formers, there was also the summer migration of ambitious lower sixth formers who wanted to know about General Paper 4 – a bona fide option for Oxford University's entrance and awards papers that required no revision of any body of knowledge, just the ability to write well in response to some logic problems. Heraclitus had become the acknowledged school authority in cracking these problems from past papers, and in providing hints and clues to help boys get the hang of them. Only ever boys, so far – he'd have liked it if more girls had shown an interest. But he also enjoyed the company of these boys, mainly chancers, slightly arrogant and pleasingly sharp but inevitably lazy and attracted to the idea of 'busking it' rather than undertaking a steady course of solid revision.

And then there were the promenade plays, a wonderful mix of the staggeringly precocious and the shockingly bad, but always performed in spots where the landscape could take you away from the infelicities of the dialogue whenever necessary.

But none of these things seemed to be happening this year, and as the current situation continued, it seemed less and less likely that they would. Heraclitus's contemplation of the south front tinged itself with nostalgia, and a delicious swell of sweet sadness was just floating in on a breeze when it was completely dispelled by the flutter and clunk of at least one good book hitting the floor.

Tom saved a couple more teetering tomes and turned to meet the disapproving glower of the librarian. "Sorry, sir," he stage-whispered as he stooped to pick up the occupants of the floor. "Actually..." he put one of the books down and approached the dragon a step or two. "Do we have *The Admirable Crichton*?"

"Try the collection of J.M.Barrie plays – if you haven't just destroyed it."

Tom saw with alarm that the book that had just fallen off the top shelf of Drama and still lay sprawled on the floor did, indeed, have the word 'Barrie' on it. "Oh, thank you, sir." He picked it up, brushed it off in unconvincing but apologetic fashion, and looked through it vaguely while drifting towards the watching Heraclitus. "No, no – I don't think so." Heraclitus waited. "Does that mean it's not much good? If it didn't make the collection?"

Heraclitus was intrigued to be asked about this play and J.M. Barrie. It all seemed a bit quaint these days for the sophisticates that the Bramblingums supposed themselves, not entirely without reason, to be. "Not necessarily."

"What's it about?"

"The butler did it," replied Heraclitus mischievously, "because when the chips were down, he was the only one with the requisite capabilities. Why the interest?"

"Something Mr Fry said," Tom explained. Surely Mr Fry's favourite play wasn't a whodunnit? Heraclitus was holding out on him. So he explained about the interview, and the question. He became convinced that Heraclitus might give him something. Not just something that would save him the bother of tracking down and reading the play – something more. So he paused and watched the old guy to see if he was going to speak. And when he didn't, he tried talking a bit more, and then he paused again. Eventually he grew worried. Heraclitus made a rasping noise, as if he couldn't breathe properly. The eyes twinkled – even more than usual, perhaps – but there was a rheumy seepage out of the corner of one. "Are you alright, sir?" But Heraclitus just wheezed. The eye opened a tiny bit wider and a tear slid out and on to his nose. The mouth opened slightly in a kind of gasp that just kept coming. 'Oh, god,' Tom thought, 'it's some kind of death rattle.' As the last breath of a Brambling legend leaked on and out, the death mask moved forward, and Tom was in a panic that this colossus of college tradition was about to fall forward into his arms, and he would drop him. His eyes were distracted from the terrible face by a movement: the old shoulders had started shaking. Dust arose from the jacket and hung in the air around him.

Suddenly, like a reverse puncture, the note changed and air seemed to rush the other way, inflating the ghastly spectre before him for a second before returning once more to the final exhalation. Tom was struck by an epiphany: Heraclitus wasn't dying – he was laughing. Hard.

Supper in Paradise

It was an odd day: in places he could normally pass unnoticed, Tork was suddenly flagged down and engaged in conversation, but back in the design workshops it was the reverse. Alex and Chris and even Gareth, all three of whom more normally expressed an anxiety to see him there, now spent their time suggesting that surely he was too busy for this, and that they could cover, and that he should go. Even the farm had seemed surprised to see him. And now that he was arriving at the dining hall, he saw instantly that Geoff, the caterer, was waiting in ambush, his apparently casual stance radiating his intention to intercept him.

"Everything okay, Geoff?" Tork figured they may as well get on with it.

"You never bring Eve and Dylan with you."

Tork paused. "No. No, they're fine, thanks, Geoff. We tend to do a massive shop then nothing for weeks, and we'd just done one, so still some stuff left in the cottage."

Geoff held his hand up. "Wait there," he said, and disappeared. Tork, caught, waited. Geoff reappeared with something wrapped in plastic. "Take these, go home, have a barbecue – you can't have eaten with them for ages. Brambling can manage for a few hours. Your family need you too."

Tork fumbled. "Thanks, but I... what is it?"

Geoff shrugged. "Just four burgers from the freezer, but they're good quality steak. I was going to break them up and put them into something, but just four of them won't really make any difference, and it's a shame to waste. They'll be really good off a barbecue. I've put a couple of the softer bread buns in, and you've got some lettuce in your garden, haven't you?"

"If the rabbits and slugs have left any."

"Go on, then," Tork looked uncertain. Geoff insisted. "Off you go."

Tork relented. "Sure?"

"Of course."

"Well, okay – that would be great. Thanks. Thanks very much." Touched and surprised, Tork smiled, lifted the package as if to show it to him, turned and left.

He had an easy, fast gait and took the most direct route, but it still took him almost fifteen minutes to walk home. He finished Dylan's bath time while Eve grilled the burgers, and they ate in the garden while Dylan looked for some fresh dirt to put on. They watched him sift the soil under the hedge.

"It's been good here, hasn't it?" Tork suddenly asked. "You've not been bored?"

"No," Eve halted the progress of her burger and bun to her mouth, "no, it's been wonderful. So good to have this time with Adds, and just get some reading done when he lets me. And I've been thinking, actually: I've enjoyed teaching those two kids. Maybe I'd be better teaching kids than looking for university posts."

"You think?" She gave a 'maybe' back and forth of the head as she chewed her mouthful. Tork thought for a moment. "Which kids were these?"

She put the burger down. "I told you – James and Charlie. I don't think I know their surnames. Is James called Redmund? They're doing a project on the szlachta. Or one of them is." He didn't really reply. They ate. "They mentioned something about an epidemic?" The sun winked through the trees, preparing to sink below the Gothic Temple, and Adds picked up a worm and examined it. They watched him raise it closer to his face.

"Don't eat it, Adds," said Tork. He and Adds looked at each other. Adds was considering his father's words. "Unless," Tork added, "you really, really want to." Adds lifted the worm closer. Tork wrinkled his nose. "Yuk." Adds watched him a second longer.

"Yuk!"

Tork melted into a big smile. "Yuk!"

"Yuk!"

"Yuh-huh-uk!"

Adds put the worm in his mouth.

"No!" Eve was across the grass, her finger in his mouth, and out it came.

"Yuk!" said Adds.

"Too right," she replied as she picked him up. "But Daddy's burger..." she broke off a little and popped it into his mouth "...is much better."

"Oy," said Tork.

The sun sank a little more, and Tork sat on while Eve took Adds to bed, then reappeared. "Okay to do a bedtime story?"

"Yup – I'll do it before I go."

"You've got something on?" He looked at her, but said nothing. She sat next to him. "Something to do with this epidemic?" He just held her look. "But we don't talk about it until it's over, right?"

He looked troubled. "It's not a rule..."

"But it's what's worked for us so far." He nodded. "Well, I'll look forward to it," she said happily.

"It's not all good." He looked at her, then away. "Sometimes you're in role and the plot develops unexpectedly and you don't like your own response."

She shook her head. "Later or now, but let's not do this half-way thing." She remembered his earlier words. "You said it's been good here – past tense – are we moving on, then?"

"Is that okay?"

"We're not in trouble, are we? Has something gone wrong?"

"No, no." He gazed at the trees around them. "But I'd like to do some work with the Prune, and I suppose you and Adds need to get back into civilisation – nurseries, universities, schools, toddler support groups..." He turned. "Back to London?"

"Okay." She looked around. "It's been beautiful, but actually I'm not sure about another winter."

"It *was* cold."

"And dark – and much lonelier. I just wondered if you'd want to do one more year."

Tork opened his mouth to reply, but the voice that rang out was Adds', "Book!" They both immediately laughed at the imperious tone, and Tork got up to go in.

Another perspective

Having found no-one at the Head's office, Alison drifted indecisively out on to the south front and hovered a while. She looked around, then wandered up the steps to the magnificent portico, which commanded a view that swooped down to the lake then climbed up to the arch a mile distant on the horizon. It caught her breath, as ever, and she lingered there.

As if her need had conjured him, the distinctive head of red hair appeared rising from the corner where the trees met the lake, and as he climbed the manicured grass hill into view, his equally distinctive lope filled in below. She watched him draw level with the giant cedar tree, then began to saunter down the steps in order to intercept him on his way to the office.

Tork recognised the now familiar style of ambush. "Hi, there, Alison – you wanted a word, didn't you?" He stopped. "Wonderful evening."

"Yes." Alison came down the last two steps. "How are you holding up with all this responsibility? I mean not just today – you've being doing loads since this all started, haven't you?"

Tork gazed at her. "How am I holding up?" He turned so he was standing by her, both regarding the vista before them. "Honestly, maybe guiltily, I've been loving it. Not the acting head thing, but until then... having the farm brim-full of busy Bramblingums, growing and tending stuff, often under the leadership of my previously overlooked regulars, Paul pootling about on his three-wheeler, it's just been great. And the workshops – expanding, busier, more purposeful and real, more inventive..." He turned and faced her a second. "Terrific."

She shook her head and shrugged her shoulders, baffled. "Great. That's okay, then."

"You?"

It was difficult to form an appropriate response. "Not so much, I'm afraid. I mean I appreciate your utopian picture, it's just not been my experience. Nelson House is fraught – I mean it's as tight as a wire. They're desperately worried and it comes out in these flashes of unprovoked anger. There may have been an initial sort of honeymoon period, with the bread-making and so on, but they're on the edge of hysteria now, and it's really quite worrying." She wondered briefly if she'd had a bit of an unprovoked outburst of anger herself.

Tork expressed concern with his face but, Alison felt, less so with his words. "Do you think it's a girl/boy thing?"

"Don't kid yourself!" she retorted. "They're not as different as you'd think." He looked a bit dazed. "Do you know James Redmund?" she asked. "Third form, bubbly, happy little chap. Tight with Chelmsford Charlie, if you know him – it's a great partnership..." for a second she tried to convey the mix of James's warmth and Charlie's acuity, but then returned to her main point. "He's a happy boy, with a good friend and an older brother in the school, and he's just sobbed his heart out in my room, and he barely knows why." Tork looked equally uncertain. "He's worried sick about his parents, about..." she waved her arm expansively, "about everything out there."

Tork, stunned, simply stood and took it on the chin. Alison stopped. "I'm sorry – I didn't mean..." She didn't quite know what she hadn't meant. They stood in silence for a moment. Unwelcome news coursed through Tork and drained away his bounce. He'd suffered a puncture.

"Is that what you wanted to see me about?" Tork eventually asked.

"Oh, sorry – no." She kicked herself back into normality. "It's the camera. It wipes itself every day, doesn't it? I mean every time I restart it?"

Tork nodded. "It's only got enough memory – think of it as a tape-recorder – for an hour or less. When you restart it, it sort of records over the previous version." She absorbed this. "What's the problem?"

"It's a bit odd. This morning, I was just playing with it, really – there was nothing from last night that I wanted or anything. But I had a quick look anyway. And there was this image, definitely, of Anna Staveley." Tork looked unsure of the point. "She's a daygirl – hasn't been here for almost two weeks." There was no sign of any explanation in his face. "Could it have been some sort of echo from an older recording?"

Tork contemplated. "Not really. Especially after all this time – how often have you used it?"

"Every time I'm on duty, three times a week – so maybe four times since Anna was last here."

They looked at each other, turned away, checked round the south front, but no answer came.

"Did anything else on the tape confirm that it was shot last night?"

Alison was sure. "Yes, Fiona and Liz had a bit of a fight outside the front door – same clothes and everything."

Another pause. "Sorry, then – no idea. Except that Anna was here – where was she?"

"The classroom corridor – the same shadows in which the boys tend to lurk."

"Was it a clear image?"

"It was Anna," Alison gave enough force to the assertion to pre-empt any 'you must have been mistaken' conclusion.

"I wonder if some of them have managed to sneak in and out?" Alison said nothing. "Okay, well thanks for letting me know – maybe keep me posted?"

"Of course."

They stood for a second. Tork seemed to have trouble getting himself going, but eventually moved off.

Wide games

No moon and much activity: the difficulty was discerning wildlife from boy. Charles blinked into the dark under the trees beyond the haha. You had to be really close before you turned on your light, otherwise they'd just run, unrecognisable. And meanwhile you'd have given away your position. The real question, though, was who they were. They could be poacher-looter-thieves from town, but Charles felt in his bones that they were Bramblingums.

It seemed remarkable and pretty much incomprehensible that they'd be out at night up to no good in present circumstances, but that was boarding school boys for you, as far as Charles was concerned. Never mind that there's a lethal virus out there, we've a stash of fags and vodka somewhere. Or maybe it was just fun to come out and get the CCF to chase you: they were probably the mates of his own troop.

Disheartened, Charles decided that the crunch of dried leaves and rotten twigs he thought he'd heard was not, despite his best stealthy efforts, going to be followed up with the sound of voices or footsteps. He uncrouched and walked back towards his soldiers near the iron gate south of the lake.

Tom and the others were there waiting. "Anything, sir?"

"No," Charles shook his head. They held their rifles and looked around the darkness, straining eyes and ears. There seemed no wind, and yet the tree branches leaned and rippled their leaves a touch in the night air once in a while. A scurry in the undergrowth, too light to be the possibility of people, occasionally caught the ear; once the air-rush of predatory wings; the far-off shiver of the hoot of an owl.

"They may have gone, but let's check the trees round the church and the cedar and up to the house," Charles said in hushed tones, and they set off round the lake. Boots crunched quietly on the compounded dirt and sparse covering of coarse gravel on the surface of the track as the five of them skirted the lake over the cascades. Somehow, one ripple of the water flowing through found a tiny source of moonless starlight to reflect. It glowed off-white and gave a slight chuckle as it slipped and fell from one lake into another. The platoon passed over. Schoolside of the lakes, Charles held his hand up but, mindful of the possibility of a slapstick pile-up behind him as soldiers failed to see his sign in the dark, he also turned and spoke, "wait!"

The crunching stopped, and in the dark all five were aware of four looming forms around them, breathing. Five heads turned at different speeds and scanned the near black landscape beneath the bluer black, star-sprinkled night sky. A tiny glow of amber low beyond the great south arch indicated that the local town streetlighting was still functional. Charles peered at the arrangement of trees up the west side of the south front lawns, past the tennis courts, then across to those on the east, round the church. He wasn't sure why he'd chosen to search the east rather than the west, but could detect nothing to make him change, so decided to go with gut instinct.

"Okay," he said, and the trudging began again. They could see the water on their right, sense the space between them and the mansion on the left. Just two tiny windows shone lit from the top floor of the distant building, though a lower glow suggested that some ground floor lights, still hidden from them by the slope, were also on.

Charles stopped them again at the tip of the triangle of trees. "Ben, Archie, go very slowly up this side, staying under the trees, but keeping watch of the lawns – there will be a bit of light on them as we get nearer the mansion – so you can see anyone who tries to cross them – okay?" He sensed and just about saw them nodding. "Go really slow – you need to keep in line with us and you're travelling over much easier ground. Tom…" For a second he wasn't sure if he was talking to the right one, but Tom moved his head to listen and became more recognisable, "take Lumen up the other side – the far side of the church. I'll go through the trees themselves. If anyone hears me coming, they'll come out the sides for you to try and apprehend. Okay?"

It was all okay. The two pairs slunk away and Charles picked his own way up the slope. Once properly under the trees, uncleared undergrowth from last year clung to his feet and roots tried to topple his footing, but it wasn't too bad and he stayed pretty quiet. He couldn't sense the presence of his soldiers, and hoped that they hadn't gone too fast. It was darker than he had anticipated, but he remained aware of the lighter atmosphere over the lawns on his left, and it wasn't a large area, so he calculated that he must be nearing the church, when a voice barked out on his right.

"Halt! I mean it, halt!"

Not the sound of a scuffle, exactly, just feet crashing about.

"Were you *actually* going to rugby tackle me?" As he turned on the torch, Charles recognised that voice. The beam swept around and picked out Brendan Weeks, Head of Brass and Woodwind.

"Sir?" Tom called towards the torch.

"Alright, Tom – I've got it."

He walked a little nearer. Brendan's glasses flashed in the torchlight, and Charles pointed the beam just to the side of the dazzled face, to see him without glare.

"Charles, is it?" Brendan asked.

"Brendan, what on earth are you doing here?" Charles began. "Okay, Tom – I'll meet you on the south front," he added, encouraging the boys to leave.

Brendan watched Tom move on. "Sorry to interrupt your manoeuvres, Charles – I just needed to leave something in the church."

Charles was dumbfounded. "What?" he spoke sharply.

Brendan's interrogatory eyebrow shot up from under his glasses to assume its characteristically raised position. "Oh, come on,

Charles... the school has a habit of altering the timetable on a whim, but wind players can't just miss lessons at the drop of a hat, you know."

"What?" Charles was shocked into dumb reiteration.

"It's the musculature of the embouchure and breath control – miss two lessons and that could be four weeks without proper practice. You don't catch the first fifteen being asked to play without fitness sessions, do you?" Charles, unseen behind his torch, simply gawped. "So the students know to come to Queen's Temple and see what the arrangements are whenever there's a sudden..." he waved his hand, "a sudden *thing*."

The power of speech returned to Charles. "Are you mad, Brendan? Are you quite, quite mad? Are you seriously telling me that..."

Brendan cut him off. "Wow, Charles, you are *good* at this. Okay," he changed tone, "I'm deeply sorry to have put the boys, and indeed the whole community, at risk from the raging disease of the outside world through my irresponsible behaviour. I shall return home immediately, and probably lash myself."

Charles was momentarily transfixed by that ironic eyebrow dancing in the torchbeam above Brendan's flashing glasses, struggling to process the words and the tone, when he heard Ben's voice from behind, on the south front lawns. "Sir, sir – it's Miss Lawrenson, sir..."

Charles turned, wavered, turned back. Brendan was already walking away, looking back at him and waving his fingers in a mocking salute. Charles left it and got through the trees to the open space as quickly as he could. Alison was standing there, Ben hovering next to her.

"Charles, have you seen any sign of Anna Staveley?"

Charles flicked the torch briefly towards Ben and Archie. "Okay, boys, thank you. I'll see you at the foot of the steps." They nodded and walked away.

"Sorry if I…" she shrugged. "I'm just really unsettled by this. First she appeared on the camera thing Tork set up, then tonight I swear I caught her heading across chapel court. I thought she'd come this way."

Charles didn't quite get it. "Anna…?"

"She's a day girl – no business being here."

Things were getting away from him. "She doesn't play the clarinet, does she?"

"What?" Alison was reacquiring her irritation with him.

"I've just met Brendan Weeks. It seems he's been coming in all the time to give students their bloody woodwind lessons."

Alison couldn't read Charles' face with so little light around. "Really? What? But why would he risk that?"

Charles flicked the torch, then shone it on the grass at their feet. "I don't know. The whole thing seems to be breaking up, doesn't it? And Brendan was odd about it – but I never quite know when he's being ironic: he just seems naturally subversive, even when he isn't."

The two of them stood in silence. Alison wanted to ask him more about it, but also didn't. "I'm still furious with you, by the way."

Charles sighed. "Do you teach a bottom set?"

"Is this a prepared speech?"

"Yes."

"Okay, then – yes, I have a bottom set – fourth form."

"Well, you know sometimes you're one to one, and you think he's just thick: he can't get it. And then he says something cynical or sarcastic, and looks sideways at his mates. And you get a glimpse of something else – that he doesn't *want* to get it. He's built this witty, laddy persona and a bunch of mates out of his antipathy for academia, and now he doesn't want to give that up. If he did get it, he'd be expected to take an interest, try harder. Have you felt that?"

Alison considered. "A bit. More usually with the girls: they think being rubbish at maths is a crucial part of their femininity, and they won't give that up. Drives me mad."

"That's an even better example – that's just it." It was somehow easier for him to talk like this in the dark. "You see I'm a bottom set slow learner here: I can understand feminism or whatever you want to call it, I think, just about, on an intellectual level, but I'm a young male history teacher with a privileged position and a professional expertise in the way the world was – two thousand years of cultural tradition and history, of which I'm the product, in which I'm the specialist, through which I move with ease." He looked directly at her, although it made little difference. "It's my element, and it's a lot to give up. But I'm trying."

Alison said nothing at first. "So you're a beautifully evolved fish that's just learning that the water's toxic?"

Charles laughed. "Okay, that would probably have been better. Apology accepted?"

She started walking away. "I'll think about it."

Abdication

The morning was as delicately beautiful as ever as the sun strengthened on Tork's progress through the field and into school, later than usual. He didn't go into the main building and Elizabeth, with her back to the window, didn't see him go past. He went on to the workshops, but he was just filling time, really. Then he set out back to the Head's house. There were one or two boys already at the chapel entrance as he passed.

Jenny Linklater looked concerned to see him. "He's barely up," she said. "Is everything alright?"

She opened the door for him. "Thanks – I'll only keep him a second. The news should be a relief to him." She led the way to the kitchen, where Whitley was sitting unnaturally upright at the table, a cup of coffee in front of him. "Not horizontal?" Tork asked him.

"Take a seat," Whitley gestured.

"Would you like a cup of coffee, Tork?"

Tork held up his hand. "No, thanks, Jenny. I'm just on my way to assembly."

"I've been horizontal all night," said Whitley. It's good to have a moment or two upright, then I'll go down again."

Tork nodded. Jenny withdrew.

"You're looking better – all doped up?"

"Oh, yes. But I think the healing process is beginning, thank you."

Tork left just a second's pause, and decided to get on with it. "I'm having an assembly, and I've just nipped in to tell you what I'm going to say." Whitley felt no comment from him was expected at this point. "I'm going to tell them that I've been enormously proud of them this last couple of weeks, and the simply superb way that they have responded to the many challenges, and of their team spirit – and I know that the Headmaster feels exactly the same way?" He looked enquiringly, and Whitley nodded. "Very well done, I shall say. But that's enough, and it's now time to return to normal." He looked very directly at Whitley, and put particular emphasis on the next few words. "I was tasked to put the school through a national emergency drill, and that's what we have been doing. There is no epidemic: it was a practice. Your families are fine, always have been, and were informed about this drill. You have shown we can respond brilliantly to an unexpected crisis, and you have also taken part in a terrific, participatory, live, real-time, improvisational, reality drama. Thank you." He paused, holding Whitley's eyes, shrugged. "That's it." He made a face. "Sorry."

They looked at each other a few seconds longer before Whitley spoke. "One or two members of staff have asked me to consider this possibility of late, even offered some evidence." His eyes flicked down to the table and back up. "But I said I trusted you."

"I'm sorry." Tork placed a sheet of paper on the table. "This is the letter you sent to all parents and off-site staff, posted to arrive the day of lockdown," he said. Whitley glanced at it. "I should be able to get the telephones, tv and radio working about half an hour after assembly," Tork added. "We owe a couple of our tenant farmers money, but we should have saved a bit on our usual suppliers." He got up. "I hope you'll agree to confirm this version of events – it would save embarrassment, I guess. But it's your call, obviously." He paused. "Anyway, I'll send Ian and Phil to see you after assembly, shall I? Actually, perhaps just Ian. Phil's a bit, well, needy, isn't he?" A ghost of a smile flickered on Whitley's lips. "Anyway, he'll have a *lot* of mail to work through – you should see it..." He attempted a humorous smile. "Well, I'd better go. Sorry and... see you." He walked into the corridor. "'Bye, Jenny!" he called, then left.

Brick was waiting for him on the Chapel steps, chiding a couple of latecomers as they scooted in. "All set, Headmaster," he said.

"Speaking of whom," Tork replied, "would you pop down and see him straight after we're done?"

"Of course," said Brick, as Tork swept straight past him and down the aisle between two large masses of humanity that fell silent and came to their feet as he walked.

There then followed the shortest Headmaster's assembly in Brambling history. Tork said exactly what he'd said he would, and it took him seventy-five seconds. He then added. "It's only a few days until half-term, and then we have exams, so it's back to work as quickly as you can. That is all."

He came round the podium and the school were a little slow to react, coming to their feet hesitantly. But he did not process down the aisle anyway, he swung left, through the side door, and off to his box of tricks on the roof.

A couple of days later, Whitley walked very gingerly and with a peculiar posture up the path to the workshops. He wasn't even through the door before he'd detected that it wasn't the same place as it had been for his last visit, although it still had an attractive atmosphere. The timetable had reasserted itself, and all the boys were of an age, and there was an increased uniformity about their activities. But they were getting on happily with their projects, and Alex and Chris looked well in control.

They acknowledged his presence politely, but as he was unable to stoop down to look at anyone's work, he didn't ask anyone about what they were doing. He simply caught Alex's eye and asked, "Tork?"

Alex indicated the back, where Tork and Rahman could be seen sitting at a pair of computers, and Whitley shuffled towards them.

"Headmaster!" cried out Tork, with genuine warmth. "How terrific to see you! Come and look at this," he beckoned him, "over here…" Whitley complied, not without discomfort. "Watch this! Go on, Rahman."

Rahman pressed a few keys, and a green dot appeared on his screen. He hit one final key, and the dot started tracking across. Another dot appeared on Tork's screen, and it, too, tracked across in the same way. Tork pressed a few keys on his keypad, then he, too, struck a final one. First Tork's dot, then Rahman's, appeared to reverse. "Ha! Nice one, sir!" Rahman and Tork slapped hands. Rahman got up and looked from Tork to Whitley and back again. "Actually, sirs, I've got to get to Physics, if that's okay."

"Good idea," said Whitley. Rahman left. Tork gazed on at the screen. Whitley asked, "What have I just seen?"

Tork looked at him. "Computers talking to one another."

Whitley nodded. "Like telephones?"

Tork was patient. "*People* talk to each other *through* telephones. This is more like me telling my telephone to explain to your telephone what it needs to explain to you."

"The difference escapes me."

Tork smiled, paused, shrugged, drew a verbal picture. "Somewhere, a guy like me is showing to a guy like you something just like this. Only the guy like you has just a little more imagination, and those two..." he repeated it for emphasis, "*those two* are going to be super rich."

Whitley decided he wasn't going to seek to understand this enigmatic little teaser. "Tork, we need to have a meeting. Can you come now?"

"It's tempting," Tork grinned. "God, I used to love those plays. Finally, the difficult protagonist meets the power figure for the big interview that brilliantly articulates the themes... Actually, one of the best is from a novel. You know *Brave New World*?" Whitley nodded. "When Mustapha Mond tells Jon Savage that if he wants freedom he's going to have to have illness, and death..."

"And misery, and suffering, and..."

"And Jon says, 'I claim them all'..."

"'You're welcome,' said Mustapha Mond."

"That's *right*!" Tork leapt up and would have slapped hands had Whitley had a better back. "You'd make a great Mustapha Mond. You'd say something wise about responsibility making great men small, but also vice-versa, and I'd rage about education, and you'd tell me that you had to let me go."

Both froze. Whitley nodded. "We need to talk."

But Tork smiled. "No. Two reasons. One – you changed the script. You went for a walk, saw my version of your school, appreciated it, talked to me, and then... then you went and made me *be you* for a spell. All that made a big final meeting a bit redundant. And two –

I'm not so keen on those plays now: I prefer the ones that leave the audience to draw their own conclusions."

Whitley saw the point, but there was one part of this final meeting that he had to insist on keeping. "I have to let you go."

"You do! I've already got another job." Slowly, Whitley nodded. "Actually," Tork continued, "we thought we'd just pack up and leave over half term."

Whitley nodded again, smiled a little sadly, turned to go. Then, as if in a scene from a film, he turned and looked back over his shoulder to say one last thing before his exit: "It's been fun, right?"

Epilogue

Brambling College Alone, the film that Tork and Prune made, showed on BBC2 in 1979, and was watched mainly by educationalists. But the papers liked it, and were excited by its innovative fly-on-the-wall fixed camera techniques, easy on voiceover, using what they called 'a kind of reality drama narrative' instead. It generated so much discussion, not least about the ethics of watching people who did not seem to know they were being filmed, that it was shown again in a prime time slot on BBC1 in 1980. By this time other questions had arisen. The school had refused to acknowledge the film, saying that it was the work of a troubled but creative member of staff no longer in their employ, but some off-the-record interviews backed up the claim that it was based on a real exercise that senior staff implemented, whereas others did not. Some of the film itself appeared to undercut the idea that senior staff knew what was going on, including a splendid scene filmed by a camera in a corridor when the Head's secretary angrily disperses a group of housemasters.

So great was the controversy that the film was given a repeat broadcast only two months later, after which the school experienced a huge growth in enquiries. By the time Whitley Linklater, sometimes unkindly and unfairly remembered as Witless Lacklustre, retired, he was able to hand on a school full to bursting with a long waiting list of aspirant Bramblingums. His successor, correctly anticipating the advent of computerised league tables, introduced selection based purely on exam-passing ability, and the school now flourishes in the top twenty of those lists. Alison is the Deputy Head with special responsibility for pastoral care in what is now a wholly co-educational school. Incidentally, she is married with children. Charles married a banker two years after being headhunted by a Brambling parent for a role in the city, where he forgot everything he had been about to learn, and his wife had to start his lessons again from scratch.

Tork only worked with Prune for the one film, then got a job lighting operas for two seasons. He, Eve, Dylan and little brother Donovan now live and work in Silicon Valley.

The Brambling experiment, as it came to be known, is normally credited with having made enormous strides forward in a number of fields of development. Besides the obvious contributions to the birth of the internet, reality tv, experimental drama, gaming, high fives, small-camera use, educational theory – the list goes on – it was also the inspiration for many imaginative works including a long-running situation comedy that drew on the footage of housemasters' meetings, and, of course, it was the making of Brambling College.

Or, anyway, that's what Tork says.

Printed in Great Britain
by Amazon